WILLERTON WOODS

SUSAN L. PARE'

Printed in the United States of America.
First Edition: March 2017
All rights reserved.

Cover designed by Susan L. Pare'

ISBN-13: 978-0-9966195-6-1

Contents

1990

One

"I'm scared."

"Be quiet, girl."

I wanna go home," she whined.

"I said be quiet."

"I'm tired. Can we go home now? It's scary here. Please, Daddy," she pleaded, "I wanna go back home."

She tripped over a root sticking up out of the ground and fell on her knees. She looked up at her father and started to cry.

"Get up right now and stop that crying," he yelled.

She tried to stand. Her legs were weak and she started sobbing, tears running down her thin little cheeks. "I can't – I can't – I can't get up," she stammered. "Help me."

Her father reached down and grabbed the back of her flimsy little coat and pulled her to her feet. "Get moving," he told her. "And, stop that damned crying."

"Daddy?"

"What now?"

"Please, Daddy, hold my hand."

Her father stopped walking and shined his flashlight on her. She held out her hand, hoping he would take it. She's so tiny, he thought. No one ever guessed her correct age, always thinking that she was younger than her five and a half years.

He ignored her outstretched hand and looked around at his surroundings. They were deep into the woods, surrounded by trees that blocked out much of the light during the day. But now it was night and the woods were pitch black. He could barely see his hand in front of his face. The girl's right, he thought. I can see how this could be scary for a little kid.

He wasn't concerned about finding his way back home. This had been his playground as a young boy. He had killed his first deer in these woods. He had never left home and he still lived in the house where he was raised, inheriting it after his father died.

His mind reflected back to the afternoon he had come home from school and found his father sitting on the front porch waiting for him. His stomach churned up and he had felt sick, knowing that something was wrong. His father was never home at that time of the day.

"Everything okay, Pa?" he had asked, as he approached his father.

"Your ma is gone, boy. She packed up and took off. I don't know where to and I don't care. That's it. I don't ever want to hear one word about her come out of that mouth of yours. Got it?" his father had said.

"Yes, sir."

His father stood up and looked at him. "That's it, then. Time to make supper."

"Daddy?"

His daughter's voice brought him back to the present. He shifted the child he was carrying to his other arm. "Get moving. We've got a way to go yet," he told her.

"Carry me, too," she begged.

"I can't, girl. Your brother is all I can handle right now. You walk."

Her crying cut deep into the silence. Suddenly,

she heard a rustling noise and screamed.

"You stop that now, you hear?"

"There's something in the woods, Daddy. Did you hear it?"

"It's nothing to worry about, Claire Ann. Now you stop that screaming."

"It sounds real close. What was it?"

"Probably a squirrel, I figure."

"Maybe somebody is lost here in the woods."

"It was just a squirrel. It's nothing to be afraid of. Let's go."

As her father started walking, she grabbed the back of his jacket and hung onto it.

"Whataya doing, girl? Why are you pulling on my jacket?"

"I can hardly see you."

"Well, just keep up. And, let go of my coat."

"Will you hold my hand?"

"I can't. You need to try to walk a little faster."

A few minutes later her father heard her fall again. He stopped and waited for her to get up. "You okay?"

"Yes, Daddy."

"Not much farther now," he told her. "Just stay behind me and keep your eyes on the light."

Her father stopped ten minutes later and looked around the clearing. He laid the boy down on the grass and glanced up at the sky. There were few clouds and the light from the moon shined down on them.

"Are we here?" she asked.

"Yes," he answered.

"It's lighter now. I can see better now, Daddy."

"Sit down and rest, Claire Ann."

The little girl reached down and felt the grass. "The grass is wet," she said.

"It's up to you. Sit or stand. Makes me no difference. Just stay where you are. I need to go check out the cabin."

"Take me with you," she begged, starting to cry again. "I don't want to stay here all alone."

"You need to watch your brother for me."

"He's asleep."

"No, he isn't, Claire Ann. I already told you that. He's dead. You killed him. Remember?"

"I didn't mean to hurt him, Daddy."

"I know you didn't. Now, you stay here and I'll be back in a few minutes to get you."

She looked up at her father and shuddered, as she felt a chill run through her little body. Somehow, she knew, at that exact moment, that it would be the last time she would see him.

She stood there, tears running down her cheeks, and watched him walk away until he faded into the darkness.

She waited, fighting her body's demanding need to sit, until her little legs could no longer hold her. Finally, she gave in and allowed her body to sink into the high, wet grass.

She crawled a few feet to her brother and pulled the blanket off of his dead body. Still whimpering, she spread out the blanket, crawled onto it, curled up into a little ball, and cried herself to sleep.

Two

The sunlight woke her. She put her little hand over her eyes and rolled away from the bright light. She was cold, thirsty and she had to pee. She stood up and looked around, hoping to see the cabin her father had told her he was going to go check out.

The desire to relieve herself became too strong to ignore any longer and she walked a few feet to the edge of the woods, pulled down her pants, squatted, and peed.

Finished, she stood up, looked over at the spot where she had slept, and suddenly realized that her baby brother was gone. The premonition that her father wasn't coming back for her had been true. She was all alone and lost in the woods.

The screeching sound of a blue jay filled the air, and she looked up at the trees, hoping to see the noisy bird. Her stomach rumbled loudly, reminding her that she was hungry.

She walked to the center of the clearing, stumbling occasionally when she stepped into small ruts. She stood there, studying her surroundings. The clearing was long and narrow and lined with tall trees. Even now, although the sun was shining, the woods were dark and menacing. Hoping to find the cabin her father had mentioned, she started to walk the perimeter of the clearing.

She cried out as the noise of a squirrel, jumping into a batch of dried leaves, scared her. She watched the little animal run across the clearing in front of her, wondering if he had a home here in the woods and brothers and sisters to keep him company.

She felt bad that her little brother, Carl, was dead. Her father said she had hurt him and that he was dead now because of her. She knew that being dead meant he had gone to heaven and she wouldn't see him again. Her grandma was in heaven, too. Sometimes she missed her and she wondered if she would miss Carl, too. She didn't think she would. He didn't talk yet or do much of anything. She didn't know him that well; not like she had known her grandma

She stopped walking when she noticed something shiny about thirty feet into the woods. She moved closer and saw that the sun, breaking through the trees, was reflecting off of something.

Excited now, thinking that she had found the cabin, she walked faster toward the shiny object. She hesitated at the edge of the clearing, afraid to go any farther. She stood there, gathered up her courage, and took a step into the woods.

Within seconds, she was standing next to an old deer blind. Although one side of the blind was gone and the branches and leaves that had camouflaged the metal roof were missing, it was still standing.

Claire Ann stared at it, wondering what it was. To her, it looked like something that a child would play in. If a child had a play house here, she reasoned, then, there should be a house close by.

She bent down and looked inside the small structure. All she saw were lots of old leaves and some small dead branches that had fallen off of trees. She crawled into it and smiled. She fit just fine.

She sat down, looked out of the open side of the deer blind at her surroundings, and realized that her rear end was getting wet from sitting on wet leaves. She crawled out into the open space and stood up. It was time to find the house where the child, who had played here, lived.

She walked into the clearing where she had spent the night and picked up her blanket. She wrapped it around her shoulders like a cape and walked back into the woods.

She soon realized that if she kept the clearing on her right and in view, she could go deeper into the woods without getting lost. She walked slowly, always looking to her left, hoping to sight the house where the child lived.

She walked the area three times, each time feeling more confident and venturing a little farther into the woods.

As a breeze swept over her, she felt a slight chill go through her little body. She glanced up at the sky and realized that dark, threatening clouds had replaced the sunlight, causing the woods to look more sinister than before.

She jumped, startled as thunder broke the silence of the forest and a bolt of lightning flashed across the sky. She heard the pattering sound of rain falling onto the leaves of the trees. She glanced around, remembered where the playhouse was and headed in that direction. She knew that, although the trees would protect her from the rain for now, it was only a matter of time before she would be wet and cold.

Within minutes she was inside the deer blind, clearing the wet leaves away. The falling patter of the rain on the metal roof was soothing and she cuddled up in her blanket and fell asleep – hungry – thirsty - and cold.

Thunder rattling overhead woke her. She was shivering and pulled the blanket around her thin body, hoping it would warm her. She looked out of the open side of the deer blind into the forest, but it was too dark to see farther than a few feet into the woods.

She needed to pee, but couldn't bring herself to crawl out of the deer blind into the scary woods. She willed her little body to hold it in, curled up, and slowly drifted back to sleep.

The sun was shining when she woke a few hours later. She didn't know what she should do next. She was afraid to go deeper into the woods, fearing she would lose sight of the clearing. Yet, she knew she had to find a way to the child's house.

She picked up her blanket and walked to the center of the clearing, turned, and looked in each direction. She wanted to go home and she thought if she went to her right, she might find her house. But, then, she remembered that it was dark when her daddy had brought her here and they had walked for a really long time. She didn't know if she could find her way back.

She was pretty sure it would be better if she went left, past the playhouse, and found the child's house. They would have food and she was so hungry and thirsty. She turned and looked in each direction again, not sure what to do or which way to go.

Scared and confused, her little body dropped down into the tall grass, tears rolling down her cheeks, and she gave in to her fears and wept.

Three

Claire Ann was hungry. She found a few berries growing on a bush and tried to eat them. But they were bitter and she spit them out onto the ground.

She satisfied her thirst after she came across a small hole, filled with rainwater. She scooped the water into her little hands and ravenously gulped it until there was nothing left.

She decided the best way to find the child's house was to walk straight into the woods, with the clearing at her back.

The weather was colder today, and although it had stopped raining, the storm clouds lingered menacingly in the sky. She pulled her coat tight against her little body and wrapped the blanket over her shoulders, trying to ward off the chill she was feeling.

She had been walking most of the morning. Her steps were getting shorter now and she was getting tired. She looked over at a fallen tree and decided it would be a nice place to rest for a while. She removed the blanket from her shoulders, spread it out on the ground, and sat down with her back resting against the fallen tree. Ever so slowly, her little body gave in to her weariness and she curled up into a little ball and fell asleep.

A chattering sound woke her. She opened her eyes and saw a squirrel standing on its hind legs, a few feet away, watching her. She wondered if it was the same squirrel she had seen the day before.

She looked up and saw that the sky was blue and the clouds had disappeared. She was glad that the weather had cleared, even though it still looked gloomy here in the woods. She hoped that she wouldn't get rained on again. Perhaps, she thought, she would find the child's house soon and she would be able to sleep in a nice warm bed tonight.

She picked up her blanket and headed out, hoping she didn't have much farther to go. She was so very hungry.

She focused on moving from tree to tree, trying to walk as straight a line as possible. Hearing a strange noise, she stopped and waited. Hearing the sound again, she turned to her right and gasped. A huge buck was standing between two large trees, staring at her. Suddenly, he snorted and pawed the ground with his front foot. She froze in place, her little heart pounding with fear. He pawed the ground again and took two steps towards her.

Her legs gave out and she went down on her knees, uttering a whimpering sound. The deer stopped, pawed the ground once more, turned, and walked away. She buried her face in her hands, and cried out, "Daddy. Help me."

She stood, her body still shaking, and continued on her way. She was determined not to rest again until she found the house. However, after hours of walking in the woods, her little body, weak from no food and little water, was again demanding sleep.

The sun was setting now, and she knew it would be dark soon and that she needed to decide on a safe spot to spend the night. Suddenly, she stopped and stared, not believing her eyes. "Nooo!" she screamed, her cry echoing through the woods.

Twenty feet in front of her was the deer blind. She had walked in a big circle. The only redeeming factor was that she had shelter for the night.

The birds were singing. The noise woke her and she covered her ears, not wanting to be awake. Her body ached from sleeping on the hard ground and her mouth was dry. She wondered if that hole had more water in it now. If she could find it again, maybe she could get another drink.

She crawled out of the deer blind and tried to stand. Her body was shaking and her legs ached. She finally managed to get upright. Standing now, she felt dizzy and tried to steady herself against the unstable structure.

She tried taking a step and hesitated when she thought she was going to fall down. After a few seconds, she took a few more steps and finally made her way to the clearing.

The tall grass was wet and, as she dropped down into it, she saw that her hands were wet from the moisture that had collected on the grass during the night. She started licking the grass around her, getting just enough moisture to wet her lips.

Claire Ann rolled over onto her back and stared at the sky. She was light-headed and confused. Her eyes hurt and she wanted to get out of the bright light.

She stood and looked around and wondered why there were so many trees in her backyard. Then, she saw her father standing at the edge of the woods, motioning for her to join him. She smiled, held out her hand, and stumbled towards him.

She walked past the edge of the clearing and into the woods, always just a few steps away from reaching her father. She fell a few times, but he was always there, waiting for her when she got up.

He led her farther and farther into the woods, until she fell to the ground, exhausted. She reached out her hand. "Please, Daddy," she sobbed, "help me."

2016

Chapter One

Jessica woke with a start. Her heart was racing and she was wet with sweat. She looked around her bedroom, but she didn't see any monsters lurking in corners or under her bed. She was safe. She took a couple of deep breaths in an attempt to calm herself.

After lying there for a few more minutes, staring at the ceiling, her pulse returned to normal. She threw her legs over the side of her bed and stood. As she walked the few steps to her kitchen, she swept her dark hair away from her face and out of her eyes.

"Damn, you scared me. It's only five-thirty. I thought you were still asleep."

"Nightmare," Jessica informed her.

"Again? What do you think set it off this time?"

"I'm not sure. It might have been all that talk about going on a picnic tomorrow."

"That might be it. Lori did suggest you guys meet at Eagle Nest State Park, and you definitely have an aversion to being around lots of trees."

"Aren't you the bright detective?"

"Have you ever considered seeing someone? You know, to find out why you keep having the same nightmare over and over."

"I'm not crazy, Suzanne."

"I didn't say that you were. But it might be a good idea to seek some professional help. Wouldn't you like to find out the reason why you have that dream and, maybe – just, maybe - get rid of the demons that cause it?

"I guess. How'd you sleep?"

"Fine," Suzanne replied. "That is one comfortable couch."

"What's on for today?"

"I'm meeting Dan. We're driving up to see his folks."

"Are you still working on the wedding plans?"

"We are. We need to finalize everything this weekend. The big day is only a few weeks away. By the way, did you go in for your final fitting?" Suzanne asked.

"I did. It's a beautiful dress, Suzanne. It fits perfectly and shouldn't need any more alterations. As long as I don't gain an ounce before your wedding, that is."

"Good. I've got to get going. Thanks for letting me crash here last night."

"Anytime. Enjoy your drive and say hi to Dan for me."

Jessica poured herself a cup of coffee and turned on a small TV, which sat on the kitchen counter. She didn't watch a lot of television, but she liked to catch the morning news. A lot of bad stuff happened in this world between the time she went to bed and got up and she wanted to be sure she was up to date on every horrifying detail.

Lately, she had been following the case of Rachel Willerton, a young woman who had been arrested and charged with killing her father. It wasn't the murder itself that was so interesting, even though patricide was considered rare. What fascinated Jessica was the way the girl had killed him. Jessica often daydreamed about killing someone and she was always looking for new ways to play out her fantasies in her mind.

This macabre side of Jessica was a side she kept hidden. To anyone who knew her, Jessica was an attractive, fun-loving woman with a fantastic sense of humor. She was kind, generous, and caring and she was always the first one to step up and help out a friend.

A few months ago, Jessica had approached a woman living on the streets and had invited her to spend the night in her apartment. The woman came willingly, grateful to have a place to stay, and trusting that she would be safe in a stranger's home.

After the woman had showered, Jessica fed her, gave her clean clothes to wear, and made up the couch for her to sleep on. There was little conversation between them, as the exhausted woman fell asleep within minutes after she crawled under the covers.

When Jessica came home from work the next day, the woman was gone. Jessica picked up a sheet of paper that had been left on the coffee table and smiled. It was a pencil rendition of her profile, with a note thanking her for her kindness.

Jessica's friends were appalled when they found out about it and made her promise not to do anything like that again. "You're lucky you're not dead," they told her. Jessica smiled and told them that they needed to trust people more, but she did promise she wouldn't do it again.

What Jessica didn't tell them was that she had

spent the night watching the woman sleep while fantasizing about all the different ways she could kill her and dispose of her body. After all, wouldn't this be the perfect victim, Jessica thought? A woman all alone and living on the streets. Who would possibly miss someone like that?

When she realized there was nothing new being reported about the young woman, Jessica turned off the TV. She was disappointed, as she was hoping to find out a few more details. For instance, what kind of saw had been used? Jessica thought it had to be some type of a power saw. She smiled, as she pictured herself standing over a man holding a big ass chainsaw. Man, she thought, that could really do a whole lot of damage.

"What the hell is wrong with me?" Jessica uttered to herself. Maybe Suzanne is right and I should see someone, she thought. These bloody thoughts running through my head are gonna drive me to drink one of these days. Or, something even worse.

She finished her coffee and headed towards the bathroom to take a shower. She was just about to turn on the water when she heard her phone ring. She hesitated, trying to decide if she should pick up the phone or let it go to voice mail. Curiosity won out and she stepped out of the shower and ran to answer her phone.

Chapter Two

"Can you hold just a minute?"

Jessica grabbed her baby blue satin robe off the end of her bed and quickly put it on.

"Sorry, about that. So, who is this? I didn't catch your name."

"I'm Peter Fisher. I've been appointed to handle the Rachel Willerton murder trial. I want to tell you upfront that the reason I'm calling is that I'm in way over my head and I want out. I think, if I can get a replacement, the judge will go along with my request to take me off this case. I was wondering if you would agree to take over. I know it's a lot to ask, but I checked around and your name kept coming up as the best attorney around here to handle this case."

Jessica couldn't believe what she was hearing. This was going to be one of the biggest murder trials ever. Maybe, even bigger than the O.J. trial and this idiot wants out.

"Are you sure? You're all over the news right now. This case could make you famous, Peter."

"This case will kill me. I'm not experienced in this field. Hell, I just passed the bar a couple of months ago. I still don't know why the judge picked me. I guess I was in the wrong place at the wrong time. I can't represent her and do a decent job. Plus, Jessica, I'm positive she's guilty as sin and I think she should get the death penalty."

Jessica didn't know Peter Fisher. However, from what he had just told her, he was certainly right about abdicating from this case. Guilty or innocent, Rachel had the right to a fair trial and Fisher wasn't going to make that happen.

"You still there?" Fisher asked.

"Sorry. I was thinking about what you said."

"You'll do it then?" Fisher inquired. "I know I'm asking a lot, this being pro bono and all, but look at all the free publicity you'll get. Plus, just think if you get her off. You'll have so much work, you'll be turning dozens of potential clients away from your door. You'll be rich and famous, Jessica. Trust me, you should do this."

"Hold up, Fisher. I'm doing just fine right now and I certainly don't need a loser murder case to make me famous. If you think she's guilty as sin, why not just plead her out and get it over with?"

"She won't agree to a plea. She swears she's innocent, even though they found enough evidence to convict her ten times over. She wants her day in court, on the stand."

"Do you think it's wise to let her testify? That's never a good idea in cases like this."

"I know. But I have to allow it if she demands it. Please, Jessica, I'm not up for this. What do you say? Will you help me get out of this?"

"I'm not saying yes, but....."

"Thank you. Man, I feel like a million pounds was just lifted off my shoulders."

"I wasn't through. I'm not saying I will take it. However, I'm not saying I won't. Before I make a decision, there are a few things I need to know."

"Anything – just tell me and it's done."

"Peter, please let me finish before you interrupt

me again."

"Sorry."

"First, I want to meet you and go over Rachel's file. I want to see everything you've got so far."

"It's not much. I...."

"Wait. I'm not done. Then, I want to meet Rachel. I need to talk to her before I decide anything. I need to get a feel of what I'd be dealing with."

"Good. Anything else?" Fisher asked her.

"Yes, if I agree to help, I would come on as co-council. You're not off the hook. You would still be attorney of record and help work the case."

"I don't understand. Why would you need me?"

"Well, for starters, you'll be paid by the court, so you can bill out some of the expenses. Win or lose, the experience you will get is priceless. And, I can use someone with a legal background to help out with the everyday stuff. Although, I'm sure one of my paralegals would do a better job than you."

"Thanks for that."

Jessica laughed. "Well, Peter, from what you've told me so far, I'd say it's probably true."

"Probably," Fisher muttered. "So, what's next, then?"

"Let's meet at the jail, so we can go over what you've got and I can meet Rachel. If I agree to help you, then we can try to get before the judge first thing Monday morning. Is two o'clock tomorrow good for you?"

"It is now. Thanks. You have no idea how much I appreciate this."

"There's one other thing, Peter."

"What's that?"

"If we represent Rachel, we fight for her. I don't care if you do think she's guilty. You're going to do everything in your power to get her off. Understand?"

"I hear you. I think I can do that."

"Well, you better think long and hard about it, Peter. Because, if I suspect that you're not giving one hundred percent, I'll leave you hanging and walk away without giving it a second thought."

"I understand."

"You better understand, because I'm serious about this. So, do you think you can do that"

"I can and I will, Jessica. Thank you."

"Don't thank me yet. There's a very good probability that you're gonna hate my guts before this is over."

Jessica couldn't believe her luck. She knew the minute Fisher asked her to step in that she would do it. This would probably be the most gruesome murder trial that she would ever be a part of and she couldn't wait to see the crime scene photos. The news stations wouldn't even show them, saying they were too disturbing.

Now, she was going to be right in the middle of it all, representing a girl who had been arrested for one of the goriest murders ever. She would finally know all the details firsthand.

Smiling, she let her robe fall to the floor, and stepped into the shower, letting the hot water wash over her body.

Chapter Three

Rachel Willerton decided she needed a different attorney. The idiot that had been appointed by the judge to handle her case was exactly that. An idiot! Rachel didn't have a lot of smarts when it came to the law, but she knew bad when she saw it, and this guy was bad.

She knew that her attorney, Peter Fisher, was fresh out of law school and had just recently passed his bar exams. At this point, most of the cases he had tried were simple traffic violations or civil suits. When it came to a first-degree murder case, like hers, he was way out of his realm of expertise.

Rachel's cellmate, Peggy, had told her that she could request a different attorney. However, she would have to inform the judge that she wanted to fire Fisher and the judge had to sign off on her request. Unless she had a good reason, Peggy had said, he might not agree to her changing lawyers and might not assign her a new one. I don't think having a lawyer who hasn't had a lot of experience is gonna be a good enough reason, Peggy told her.

Peggy had also told her that she could hire a different attorney if she had the money to pay for his services. Rachel barely made the rent money that she had to pay her father each month, so she knew that was a no-starter. Of course, now that he was dead, she didn't have to worry about rent money.

She decided to risk it with the judge and request

that he assign her a new guy to handle her case. Her life was a stake and she certainly wanted someone who would fight for her in court.

Peter Fisher had suggested she strike a plea deal for a lighter sentence and forget about a jury trial. Rachel had gone a little crazy when he said that and kicked his sorry butt out of the room

It was Saturday and she had nothing else to do but to try and figure out how to approach the judge. Should she ask Fisher to accompany her and make the request, or could she ask to talk to the judge alone? She had no idea what to do, but she did have the weekend to talk to some of the inmates and get advice. A number of the women here were repeat offenders and were likely to know how the system worked.

Rachel thought she should be in juvie– not in jail. She had just turned sixteen and was still considered a juvenile as far as the law was concerned. She couldn't drink or vote yet, but for some reason, the judge had agreed to the prosecutor's request that she be tried as an adult. Rachel knew if she was tried as an adult, and found guilty, her sentence would be a lot more severe than if she was tried as a juvenile offender.

Rachel believed she would be found innocent, once all the facts came out and a jury heard her story. Besides, she really thought she might be a little nuts and she had heard that being crazy was a good defense. Maybe a new attorney could convince a jury that she was crazy for a little while and that's why she killed her father.

She looked up as Peggy walked into their cell, carrying a couple of magazines.

"What did you find to read?" she asked Peggy.

"A couple of Seventeens and a Teen Vogue," Peggy said. "They're pretty new, too."

"I hope I haven't read them. I'm so bored right now, I'd read a cookbook if I had one."

Peggy laughed and handed Rachel the magazines. "Take your pick of which one you want to read first."

"You sure?"

"Of course. It doesn't make any difference to me."

"Peggy, how old were you the first time you went to jail?"

Peggy thought for a minute. "I guess I was fourteen. I only spent a few nights in juvie, though."

"What did you do wrong?"

"Shoplifting. That's what a lot of young girls get busted for. Some judges think a couple of nights in juvie is enough to scare us straight. Didn't work for me, though."

"It didn't?"

"Nope. Obviously, or I wouldn't be in here. I was right back out there stealing everything I could get my hands on. I was sent to juvie five times before I was sixteen."

"But all you did was steal a pack of cigarettes from the drug store."

Peggy smirked. "Ya, but I'm also older now. This time, I'm in trouble, Rachel. This time they're going to teach me a lesson and I'm not getting away with just a slap on the wrist."

"Just because you stole a pack of cigarettes? That doesn't seem right."

"It's because I'm a repeat offender. I'm what they call incorrigible and I haven't learned to obey the rules. I'll tell you one thing, though. If I had known that I'd wind up here, I'd have grabbed something worth a hell of a lot more than a stinking pack of smokes."

"Like what?" Rachel asked.

"I don't know. Maybe a car or an expensive ring or something."

"Ya, like a big diamond or ruby ring," Rachel said.

"You got that right. But, now, I'm gonna wind up in jail for a friggin' pack of cigarettes. That's a real bummer."

Chapter Four

Jessica and Peter Fisher were sitting at a table in the visitation room at the county jail. They had been going over Rachel's file for about ten minutes when a door opened and they saw a correctional officer push a teenage girl into the room.

"I'm moving as fast as I can with these chains on. Shoving me isn't gonna make me walk any faster," the girl snapped at the guard.

The officer looked over at Jessica and Peter and grinned. "Are you here for this little bitch?" she asked.

"We are," replied Jessica. "And, I don't think name-calling is appropriate."

"Tell me that after you talk to her. Calling her a little bitch is being kind. There are a lot worse names I could call her.

"Maybe, you could try using her actual name next time," Jessica said.

"Whatever. You've got an hour. I don't know why you get an hour. Most of the time it's thirty minutes. You got pull around here or something?"

"Actually, we have all the time we need and we'll be here until we're finished."

Jessica waited until the correctional officer left the room, then, motioned for Rachel to sit. As Rachel walked over to the table, Jessica gave her the once over, noting that she was about one hundred fifteen pounds, maybe five feet, four inches tall, had dark brown hair with auburn highlights, and was extremely pretty.

"Who are you?" Rachel asked Jessica, as she pulled out a chair and sat down. She smiled, as she looked Jessica up and down. She glanced over at Fisher. "Is this your girlfriend, Petey? How'd a guy like you get a hot mama like this, Petey? You either have some hidden talents or one big cock. Nah, that can't be it. Wait, I got it. You must be rich. Right?"

"She's not my girlfriend. And, quit calling me Petey. I told you before that you should call me Mr. Fisher or Peter."

Jessica watched the interaction between the two of them. It was obvious that the girl had no respect for Fisher and was a little smart-ass.

"Are you two done?" Jessica inquired.

Rachel looked at her, grinning. "I guess. So, what's up with you and Petey?" she asked

"Peter, are you finished arguing with this little piece of shit?"

Rachel's head jerked up and she stared at Jessica in surprise.

Peter shook his head, indicating he was. "Sorry, about that, Jessica. I shouldn't let her get to me like that," he said. He glanced over at Rachel. "Rachel, this is Jessica Patterson. She's here to decide if she wants to take over your case. Well, not take over exactly. She might agree to be co-counsel if you can behave yourself and cooperate and she concludes that you're worth saving."

Rachel sat back in her chair, surprised. This was like a gift. She wanted a new attorney and now one just showed up. She closed her eyes, said a silent thank you to the Lord above, and sighed.

"Really? You're here to help me?"

"Perhaps. But, first of all, you'll need to understand a few conditions that I have. I hate liars. If I catch you lying to me, I won't take your case. You need to be honest and tell me everything that happened. I need all the details, even if you think they don't mean anything. I'll decide what's important and what's not important. If you think of something that happened to you that might help your case, even if you were just a little kid at the time, you need to tell me."

Jessica watched Rachel's expression change from cheeky to somber in seconds, as she realized that Jessica meant business and was there to help her. It was obvious the girl was listening and paying close attention. She waited until Jessica was done speaking.

"May I tell you something?"

"Of course," Jessica replied.

Rachel looked at Fisher. "I don't mean to hurt your feelings, but I was going to ask the judge if I could get a different attorney. I prayed for it to happen, and it did. My prayers were answered."

"You were right about wanting a new attorney," Fisher told her. "I think you need one, too."

"You do?" Rachel asked, surprised.

"Absolutely. Which is one of the reasons I asked Jessica to take your case. She will run the show, but I'll still be around to help. Rachel, if anyone can win this case, it's her. She's the best. If she agrees to represent you, you better get down on your knees every night and thank whatever god you pray to. I'm telling you she will do everything in her power to get you off. You are fortunate that she is even considering this."

"Will you do it then?" Rachel asked Jessica. "Will you help me?"

"First we talk," said Jessica. "Then I decide."

Jessica walked out of the county jail two hours later. Her head was still reeling from the interview with Rachel. The crime scene photos were some of the worst she had seen in all the years she had practiced law. She couldn't remember ever having had such a strong rush of excitement as she had just experienced.

As she walked to her car, she pulled her briefcase closer to her body, knowing that as soon as she arrived home, she would look at them again.

But, first, she wanted to take a shower. She didn't know why, but she suddenly felt dirty.

Chapter Five

Jessica's screams woke her. Her heart was pounding and she was drenched in sweat. She crawled out of bed and walked to the kitchen for a drink of cold water.

"This is the third time this week I've had that friggin' nightmare," she muttered out loud.

Suzanne was right, she thought. It's time I talked to someone. This is getting out of hand.

She glanced at the clock on the wall. Four-thirty. No sense in going back to bed, she decided. I might as well shower and head to the office. I've got a lot to do before I meet with the Willerton girl this morning.

Five hours later Jessica and Peter Fisher were waiting for Rachel to be brought into the visitor's room. Peter looked over at Jessica and was surprised at how tired she looked.

"Are you okay? You're not getting sick, are you?"

Jessica looked up from the papers she was reading. "Sorry. What did you say?"

"Are you okay, Jessica? You don't look well."

"I'm fine. I'm just a little tired. I haven't slept well this week."

"I know what you mean. This case is getting to me, too," Peter stated.

"It's not that. I'm fine with the case."

"Is it something I can help you with?"

Jessica smiled. "I wish you could, but no. I keep having this dream over and over. Actually, it's a nightmare. It seems to be happening more and more. I think I need to . . ."

Jessica looked at Peter and shook her head. "Sorry, just forget I said anything."

"What? You need to do what?"

"Never mind, Peter. It's not your problem."

"Well, if there's anything I can do, let me know."

"I doubt there's anything unless you're also a psychiatrist."

"Is it that bad?"

"It just might be. I've had the same nightmare for years now. It used to happen once or twice a month. Now, I'm having it two to three times a week. I guess I should talk to someone and try to find out what's going on in this head of mine."

"I know someone. I can give you his name if you want."

"And, he's the best in the area. Right? That's what everyone says about people they recommend."

"I'm not saying that. But he probably is the best you can do in Iron Mountain. You'd have to travel a hell of a lot farther to find anyone as good as he is. Probably Chicago or New York."

Jessica smiled. "Thanks, but I think I'll pass."

"Well, let me know if you change your mind." Peter hesitated for a couple of seconds, thinking about what he had just said to Jessica. "I'm going to give you his name anyway. You can keep it or throw it away. But, if that nightmare is anywhere near as bad as you look, I'd suggest you call him. And, soon."

Jessica suddenly felt angry at him. "Well, thanks a lot. That's just what a woman needs. To be told that she looks like. . .." She stopped talking when she realized she was raising her voice and looked at Peter. "I'm sorry. You're right. I guess I just didn't want to hear it. Thanks for your concern, Peter. And, I will take that number. Now, let's get to work, shall we?"

Rachel came bouncing into the visitor's room, a big silly grin on her face, looking like she didn't have a care in the world. She stopped a few feet away from Jessica and Peter and frowned. "Who died? You guys look like the world just ended."

Jessica looked at her. "Well, you sure are the chipper one this morning. What do you have to be so happy about?"

"Didn't you hear? I'm getting out of this stinking place. Someone paid my bond. I guess I'll be out of here in a few hours."

Jessica couldn't believe what she was hearing. There was no way this teenager knew someone who could afford to pay ten percent of her $500,000.00 bond.

"What the hell are you talking about?" Peter asked her, looking as shocked as Jessica. "Who do you know that can afford to put up that kind of money?"

"I don't know who it was," Rachel replied. "I was gonna ask you guys if you knew. All I know is that a little while ago I was told to get my stuff together and to get ready to leave. I guess my bond has been paid."

Jessica turned to Peter. "Would you go find out what's going on? Try to find out if her bond was actually paid and by whom. This doesn't sound right to me."

"I'm on it. You gonna be here or are you going back to your office?"

37

"I'm going to wait right here until you get back"

Rachel listened to their conversation, not sure why they were so upset. "I don't get it," she said. "Why aren't you happy for me? I get to go home."

Jessica looked up at her. "Sit down, Rachel. We need to talk. I think a mistake has been made. This isn't making sense."

"Why not?"

"You're sixteen years old. No judge is going to allow you to walk out of here unsupervised. You can't go back to the farm and live there by yourself. No way any judge is going to allow that to happen."

"But the jail lady said I was going to be getting out of here," Rachel whined, tears filling her eyes. "Why would she say that if it wasn't right?"

"I'm sorry. But, let's just wait until Mr. Fisher gets back, so we can find out what this is all about."

"Jessica, listen to me. I know somebody bailed me out, so I get to go home. I don't care what you say, I'm leaving."

Jessica stood up and walked over to the jailer who was standing by the door.

"Maude, is it?" she asked, looking at the name tag on the woman's shirt.

"That's right," Maude said.

"Do you have any idea what's going on with Rachel?"

"No idea. Why?"

"She thinks her bond has been paid and that she's leaving."

Maude snorted. "Sorry, but that's the funniest thing I've heard today. I don't think she knows what she's talking about. No judge is going to let her walk out of here, after what she did."

"Thanks."

"Wait a minute," Maude said, as Jessica started walking back to the table to join Rachel.

Jessica turned and looked at her. "What?"

"Maybe she's being transferred over to juvie."

"What makes you say that?"

"Well," Maude replied, "I heard that some judge decided to have one of the younger girls, being held here, tried as a minor. I didn't even consider that it might be your client, seeing as how she's in here for first-degree murder."

"You think it's Rachel?"

"It might be. We only have a couple of girls here who are under eighteen."

"But she thinks someone paid her bond."

"She probably figures if she's getting out, her bond has been paid," Maude told her.

"You might be right. Thanks, Maude."

Jessica walked back and joined Rachel at the table.

"Well?" Rachel said.

"I'm not sure. Let's just wait until Mr. Fisher gets back."

Chapter Six

Rachel finally started to settle down. Jessica gave her another Kleenex and watched as she blew her nose and wiped the tears off her cheeks.

"Are you feeling better?" Jessica asked her.

"A little."

"Good," Peter Fisher said. "We've wasted enough time here this morning."

"I did think I was getting out," Rachel said.

"You misunderstood, that's all," Jessica told her. "It could have happened to anyone."

"I guess," Rachel replied.

"Peter's right, though. We have wasted this morning and I've got to be in court in an hour."

Jessica turned to Peter and shrugged. "Not much more we can do today. Will you stay until she's transferred?"

"I can't. Plus, they won't allow me to be with her when they move her. She'll be okay on her own."

"Why can't you come with me?" Rachel asked, pouting. "I don't want to be all alone."

"You should have thought about that before you murdered your father," Peter said, sarcastically.

"I didn't do it," Rachel said, on the verge of tears again.

"I didn't do it," Peter repeated, mockingly.

"Enough, you two! Stop acting like children. Rachel, we'll see you tomorrow. Behave yourself and count your blessings. The fact that you're being moved to juvie means you aren't going to be tried as an adult."

"Really?" Rachel asked, smiling. "Are you sure?"

"I'm pretty sure. This whole morning has been a big mess. We should have been notified about this. I'm going to go speak to the judge about this and make damn sure that this isn't some kind of mistake."

"Okay. Thank you, Jessica."

"And . . .?" Jessica said, giving her an inquiring look.

Rachel looked confused for a second, then, realization kicked in and she looked over at Peter. "Thank you, too, Mr. Fisher."

"You're welcome, Rachel," he replied.

Jessica's talk with Judge Reinhold lasted less than five minutes. She caught up with him in the hallway in front of his courtroom and cornered him.

He told her that after careful consideration, being mindful of Rachel's age, he decided it was in the best interest of all parties concerned to reverse his ruling and have her tried as a juvenile.

"She just turned sixteen and I don't want a conviction verdict overturned because of her age, which is right on the line. So, I decided to err on the side of caution. She'll be tried as a juvenile," he had said.

Jessica knew that Rachel could still spend the rest of her life in prison, without a chance of parole, if a jury found her guilty. The only difference between being tried as a juvenile is that Rachel would spend the first five years of her incarceration in a juvenile detention facility, before being moved to the women's prison in Ypsilanti.

She glanced at her watch, decided she better get her butt moving and headed over to Courtroom Eight. Rachel wasn't her only client, and she had a hit-and-run case she needed to get to.

By three o'clock, Jessica had had enough. She'd been up since four-thirty and she was tired. Instead of going back to her office, she headed home. A short nap was in order before she started working on Rachel's case.

She had a load of questions for Rachel to answer when she saw her tomorrow, and she needed to start making notes. But, first, she wanted twenty minutes of undisturbed sleep. She reached for her phone and was about to hit the off button when she noticed that she had a missed call. It was from an area code number she didn't recognize.

Later, she thought. Right now, all I want is to go home and take that nap.

Nancy Fielding had hesitated, not sure if she should leave a voice mail message. She opted not to and hung up the phone. She decided she would try calling Ms. Patterson tomorrow if she could muster up the courage one more time.

She wasn't sure if she wanted to talk to Ms. Patterson, or anyone, about her reasons for leaving Jack Willerton. How could she possibly make anyone understand why she left her daughter, Rachel, years ago? How do you explain why you put your own safety before your child's? And, never look back!

Nancy turned her desk chair around and looked

out the picture window. The view of the ocean was spectacular. She loved her job. She made good money and her corner office was to die for. She loved her home, which was only a five-minute drive from her office and overlooked the Pacific Ocean. She loved her life here in Oregon. Did she really want to ruin all that now? Isn't that what could happen if she talked to the Patterson woman?

As she heard footsteps approaching her office, Nancy turned back towards the door. It was her secretary, Annie.

"Everything okay, Boss?" Annie said as she handed Nancy the mail.

Nancy smiled. "Everything's just fine."

Chapter Seven

"Are you saying that Jack Willerton isn't your biological father?"

"No. That's not what I meant," Rachel said, irritated that Peter Fisher was mixing up her words.

"But you just said your mother married Jack Willerton. So, he's your stepfather, right?"

"He's my father. My mother married him and they had me a little more than a year later."

Rachel glanced over at Jessica, who was on her cell phone. "I can't talk to him," Rachel said.

Jessica put up her right index finger, indicating that she would be with her in a minute. Rachel nodded in agreement and waited.

Jessica ended her call and turned her attention to Rachel and Peter. "All right," she said. "What's the problem here?"

"No problem," Peter said.

"Really, Peter?" Rachel asked. She looked at Jessica. "I can't talk to him," she told her. "He twists everything I say."

"Well, sometimes it is hard to figure out what you're talking about, Rachel. So, let's go over it one more time. I want you to start at the beginning and tell me the whole story," Jessica said.

"What do you mean – beginning? Start at the beginning of what? My life or from the time I got arrested? For something I didn't do, by the way."

Jessica rolled her eyes. "We'll get to the beginning of your life later. Right now, I want all the details from the time you found your father's body until you were arrested and charged with his murder."

Rachel turned away; anger written all over her face. "I didn't do it, you know. I found him like that. It wasn't me who killed him."

"So, you've said a thousand times. Rachel, I don't want to know if you did or didn't do it. All I want right now is to hear your story. Can you do that for me?"

Rachel shook her head yes and took a deep breath. "Okay. I'm ready." She didn't say anything.

"What now?" Peter said.

"Well, maybe we should take a break first," Rachel said.

"Or, maybe you should start talking and we'll take a break later. Let's hear it. Now!"

Rachel flinched as Jessica raised her voice. "Okay, I'm ready," she said, again. "But I need to tell you something else first."

Jessica and Peter hadn't said a word for almost thirty minutes. This sixteen-year-old girl had just told them the most disturbing story that they had ever heard.

Peter, realizing that his mouth was hanging open, reached for his bottle of water. He took a long swig and placed the cap back on the bottle.

Jessica licked her dry lips and swallowed. She stared at Rachel, not believing what she had just been told.

"Are you friggin' kidding me?" Jessica finally said, breaking the silence with her words.

"What?" Rachel said.

"Do you expect me to believe that story?"

"It's the truth. You can believe it or not, but that's what happened."

"You know, Jessica," Peter intervened, "it's so unbelievable that it might just be true."

"Of course, it's true," Rachel said. "Do you think I made it up? Because, I didn't."

"It's really true? All of it?" Jessica asked.

"Every last word," Rachel told her.

"So, how do we go about proving it, Peter? It's a she-said story with no proof, as far as I can tell."

"You mean she said, he said story, don't you?"

"No. The he is dead. It's only Rachel's story. No, he – just she," Jessica replied.

"Right. By the way, did you record Rachel?" Peter asked Jessica.

"Every last word. Why?"

"I'd like a copy. I want to go through this word for word. There may be something we missed. I mean, we weren't looking for clues, were we? We were just listening. I, for one, need to hear this again."

"As do I," Jessica said. "I'll get a copy to you this afternoon."

"Sounds good."

"Rachel, could you use a break? I've got some questions for you and I don't want any interruptions, once I get started."

"I'm fine."

"You sure? You don't need to use the restroom or anything?"

Rachel smiled. "Really, I'm fine. What do you want to know?"

"Well, for starters, I'd like to know where you were for three days. You said you ran away. Where were you?"

"My friend's house. I told you that already."

"Does your friend have a name? Will she or her family testify that you were staying with them?"

"Well, they weren't there."

"What do you mean they weren't there?"

"They were away on vacation."

"So, you had their permission to stay there, even though they weren't at home," Jessica stated.

"Kind of. . . I guess."

"What do you mean, you guess?"

"Well. . .."

"Well, what, Rachel?"

"I didn't exactly get their permission, but they wouldn't care that I stayed there or anything. I always stayed there when I ran away."

"Now the District Attorney can add breaking and entering to the list of charges against you."

"I didn't break anything. I had a key. I just unlocked the door and walked in."

"Where did you get a key?"

"It was under the gnome that's in their front yard. That's where they hide it. You know, in case someone gets locked out. I took it from there, so I didn't break anything. I did enter the house, though."

"And, you stayed there for three days, right? And, slept in your friend's bed and ate their food."

"Right. Mostly I ate peanut butter and jelly sandwiches."

"Why did you decide to go home? You ran away

because you were afraid of your father. So, why did you go home? Why didn't you call the police if you were so afraid?"

"Because, it was the fourth day. Whenever I ran away, I always went back home on the fourth day, because then my dad wouldn't be mad anymore. He'd be so happy to see me; he would forget what we fought about."

"How many times have you run away? Not counting this last time?" Jessica asked.

"I'm not sure. Maybe four or five."

"So, you have a pattern of doing this," Jessica stated. "That's good, Rachel. That means that you didn't run away this time because you killed your father and were afraid you'd be caught. You ran away because you had a fight with your dad and were afraid. Just like all the other times."

"That's right."

"How old were you when your father started molesting you?"

"Do I have to tell you again?"

"Please. I know this is hard for you, but I need the details."

"It wasn't too long after my mother left. Maybe, two or three months."

"You said your mother left when you were nine. Is that right?"

"I guess. Maybe I was ten."

"And, you're saying that you were only nine or ten years old when your father started to have sex with you?"

Peter, who had been listening without

48

interrupting, looked over at Jessica. "Rape. Use the word. He started raping her, Jessica. Good god, what kind of a man does that to his daughter?"

Jessica let out a sigh. "A sick one, Peter. A very sick man."

"He didn't rape me when I was ten," Rachel said. "He made me do other things. You know. Like blow jobs and touching me and stuff. He didn't have actual sex with me until I was thirteen. It was my birthday and he said I was ready for it now."

"Forcing you to give him a blow job is still rape," muttered Peter.

"Why didn't you tell someone what was going on and get help? Why did you let it go on so long?" Jessica asked her.

"Who would I tell? Besides, I was afraid of what my father would do. He said he'd hurt me if I told anyone.

"You could have gone to the police or your student counselor. What about your friend's parents?"

"I was afraid to tell anyone," Rachel replied.

"What did you and your father fight about that made you run away?" Jessica asked, changing the subject.

"You mean the last time?" Rachel inquired.

"Yes."

"I wanted to go out on a date and I needed a new dress. You know – to wear to the prom. He told me I couldn't go. He said he didn't want any dumb boy sucking my tits and fucking me. I told him that wasn't going to happen, but he still said I couldn't go. So, I ran away."

"Did your father do that?"

"What?"

"Suck on your tits. Did he do that to you?" Jessica asked Rachel.

"Sometimes. I didn't mind that, though. I kinda liked it."

Jessica sat back in her chair and stared at Rachel.

"What the hell do you mean – you liked it?"

"It felt good. So did having sex with him. It hurt when I was younger, but later it felt nice."

"What do you mean nice?" Jessica asked, hesitatingly.

"You know. When I would get off, it felt good."

Jessica stood up, walked over to the window, and looked out. It was a warm, sunny day and she could see a few juvie girls weeding the flower beds.

Suddenly, she had an urge to get the hell out of this building and never look back. She had heard enough. She didn't mind the gory details of the murder. She even got some sick pleasure out of that. But, this? This went way beyond her comfort zone.

Jessica turned back to the table, surprised to see tears rolling down Rachel's cheeks.

Rachel looked at her. "You hate me now, don't you?"

Jessica shook her head no. "No, Rachel, I don't hate you. You're a product of a mother who walked out on you and left you with a sick father who started molesting you when you were only nine or ten years old. God only knows what else went on at that farm. It's not your fault. However, you do need some

50

professional help and I'm going to make sure you get it."

"I'm not crazy, you know. What now? Are you still going to work my case?"

Jessica looked at Peter. He nodded and smiled. "Of course, we are. We're going to do everything in our power to help get you off, Rachel. Trust us. The first thing we're going to do is get a new trial date. We're going to need a lot more time to put all the pieces together before we'll be ready to bring your case before a jury," he told her.

"And, young lady," Jessica added, "the second thing we need to do is get you to a psychiatrist. If all else fails, we may have to plea temporary insanity," Jessica added.

"You do think I'm nuts," Rachel exclaimed. "I'm not crazy. I told you that."

Jessica smiled. "You did. But I think that there's a little bit of crazy in all of us, and that, my dear, includes you."

Chapter Eight

Jessica spent the night reviewing the notes she had taken during her interview with Rachel. She had listened to the recording again and continued to find it hard to believe that any child could survive living under the conditions that Rachel had experienced.

The farm, where Rachel lived, had belonged to the Willerton family since the 1800s. Jack's great grand-father had been the first of the Willertons to settle there and the land had passed down from generation to generation

Jack Willerton had been born there in 1960 and had inherited the farm at the age of twenty when his father passed away. Rachel had told her and Peter that her father barely remembered his mother, as she had abandoned her husband and Jack, when Jack was just a young boy.

Rachel thought that her father had been married before. She told Jessica that she remembered her mom and dad fighting about a woman named Marie and her father saying he didn't want to talk about that no-good rotten ex-wife of his.

Jessica decided she would send Peter Fisher to the Records Department at City Hall to search the Willerton family history. She wanted a complete history of birth, death, and marriage records. However, she knew that was going to be a difficult task. There were few hospitals back in the 1800s. Most settlers didn't even go to doctors unless they were close to death. Sometimes, the family bible was the only place where the family history was recorded.

Perhaps, there was a bible at the farm, she thought. She decided that she was going to take a look at the farm and the crime scene. The weekend was coming up and it would be a good time for a road trip. She wondered if Fisher would like to go with her.

Jessica read the CSI report again. It had taken the crime scene investigators a week before they had finished going over the property. The Dickenson County Police report was detailed, outlining where each body part had been found. Parts had been scattered over different areas of the farm and were found in the barn, the chicken coup, and the yard.

The report stated that it was extremely likely that an animal, possibly a dog or a fox, had dragged body parts to the yard from some other location. A partially chewed foot showed bite marks, probably from a dog, although no dog was found on the farm.

Jack Willerton's head and shoulders were the only parts of his body that were intact. This was probably due to the fact that Willerton had been hanging from a rafter when the lower portion of his torso had been severed. After careful examination of the corpse, it was determined that a chainsaw had been used to cut the body in half.

The report continued, stating that Mr. Willerton was most likely dead at the time his body had been mutilated. This conclusion was based on the fact that there were only small traces of blood on the floor of the barn, beneath the remains. If he had been alive at the time of death, there would have been an excessive amount of blood beneath the body.

However, the report stated that it was also

possible that some of the farm animals had consumed the blood, along with Willerton's internal organs and body parts. If that was the case, then Willerton could have been murdered while hanging from the rafter in the barn.

Jessica was confused by the report. CSI concluded he had been killed elsewhere – or – maybe, killed where he hung. She figured she might as well toss it in the waste basket for all the good it did her. Why didn't they just report that they had no friggin' idea where he was killed?

Jessica read the autopsy report next. The County Coroner stated that the exact cause of death could not be determined, as Willerton's internal organs were not found. He did report that Willerton had not died from natural causes and, considering the excessive trauma to his body, the County Corner concluded that his death was a homicide.

The police had recovered the head and upper torso, one leg, and a hand in the barn. They found a leg bone in the yard, not far from the chewed foot, and a couple of toes in the chicken coup. An arm, with multiple tattoos, was located approximately fifty yards from the house. Willerton's penis had been severed and had been rammed into his mouth and partially down his throat. His tongue, which had also been removed, was not found during the search of the grounds. The toxicology report showed no alcohol or drugs were in Willerton's system at the time of death.

Jessica opened another file and pulled out the crime scene photos and looked at them again. Each picture showed a body part and the location where it had been found.

Jessica felt the excitement soaring through her body as she studied the photos. She closed her eyes and pictured herself walking from body part to body part, stopping occasionally to bend down and faintly touch them. A shiver ran through her body and she opened her eyes.

"I'm one sick puppy," she said, put the photos back in the file, and closed it.

Time for bed, she thought, as she pushed her chair away from her desk. She picked up her wine glass and finished the small amount that was left, and walked to the kitchen. She rinsed the glass, set it in the sink, and walked to her bedroom.

As she crawled into bed, the picture of Willerton's head, hanging in the barn, flashed through her head and sent a cold shiver running through her body. She curled up into a ball and tried to fall asleep.

Jessica was a little girl, alone in a forest. It was night and it was so dark she could hardly see her hand in front of her face. Evergreens were swaying from side to side, and the rustling noise scared her.

Suddenly, the sound of thunder filled the sky. She jumped at the sound and started to cry. The rain pelted her face, making it hard for her to see.

"I want my daddy," she screamed.

Trying to protect herself from the rain, Jessica pulled the covers over her head. She slowly opened her eyes, realizing that she had just had a nightmare. Her heart was racing. Her face felt wet and when she put her hand on her cheek, she realized she was crying.

She got out of her bed and walked to her front door, checking it to make sure it was locked. Then, she walked to her kitchen and double-checked the lock on the back door, making sure it was secure.

She sat down at her kitchen table and picked up a piece of paper that she had laid there a few days ago. It had a name and a phone number on it.

She looked over at the clock on her microwave, saw it was only 4:30 a.m., and swore. It was way too early to call. But, the first thing she was going to do today, she decided, was to call that number. She just hoped that Fisher was right and that this doctor was good.

Chapter Nine

As Jessica approached the old farmhouse, she reduced her speed to a mere five miles an hour. She put her foot on the brake and slowly came to a stop. She looked around at her surroundings.

"Do you feel like we've just gone back in time about a hundred years?" Fisher asked.

"How could anyone live like this? The only thing that looks like it's been updated over time is the barn," Jessica remarked. "I've seen old log cabins before. Not all of them have been torn down. But they are usually on some abandoned piece of property and, just waiting for a good wind to blow them over. I can't believe that Rachel was raised there."

Fisher glanced over at Jessica. "You gonna get out or just sit here staring?"

"I just want to take it all in. I want to remember this moment and my first impression of this place. I want to try to imagine how Rachel could live in a dump like this and still turn out normal."

"She didn't."

"Didn't what?" Jessica asked, turning to face him.

"Turn out normal. She's nutty as a fruitcake."

"Maybe," Jessica replied. She thought for a second and continued. "One minute she seems like any other normal sixteen-year-old girl and, then, a minute later she's telling us that she enjoyed her father raping her. You're right, Peter. She's anything but normal."

Jessica opened the car door and got out. She

was glad she had worn her old boots, as the ground was wet from the morning rain, and there were mud puddles all over the yard.

She slammed the car door and started towards the house. She looked back at the car, and yelled, "You coming?" and continued walking. She pulled a key out of her pocket but realized she wouldn't need it, as the front door was slightly ajar. She waited for Peter to join her.

"The door's open," she stated, as Peter walked up to the cabin.

"You think somebody's in there?"

"No. I think the cops either forgot to lock it, or some kids have been goofing around out here and left the door open."

"You want me to go first?" Peter asked her.

"I'm fine," Jessica answered, and gave the door a push, opening it all the way.

She walked into a large room that served as the living room, eating area, and kitchen. There was a fireplace on the wall to her right, which, as far as Jessica could tell, was the only means of heating the place during cold weather.

A door, on the far wall, led to a small bedroom, which obviously had been added at a later date and was not part of the original home. Jessica stepped into the doorway and stopped, taking it all in. This was Rachel's bedroom. This was where she slept. It was also where her father had slept. Two beds, one a double and the other a twin, almost filled the room.

Rachel had said that her parents and she had shared a room and that her father continued to sleep in the same room after her mother left. However, seeing the actual room – this confined area where Rachel was continuously raped by her father - suddenly made Jessica sick to her stomach.

She turned and headed for the front door.

"Are you alright?"

Jessica shook her head no and went outside. She took a few deep breaths and waited for her stomach to settle down. Peter joined her on the little front porch and gave her an inquiring look.

"I'm surprised. I didn't think anything could get to you."

"I don't know what happened. I'm not usually like this. It's just that I got the strangest feeling that I'd been here before. Like deja vu or something. I just had to get out of there."

"Are you okay, now?" Peter asked.

"I'm fine. Sorry about that."

"Are you going back in? I thought we were going to look for a family bible."

"We are. Rather, you are. Why don't you go look for it? I'm going to walk down to the barn and check it out. Come find me when you're done here."

"Why don't you just wait for me? It's not going to take much time to look around in there."

"Fine. Go ahead and I'll wait out here," Jessica said. "Actually, I think I'll go check out the chicken coup," she told him, changing her mind.

"It's kinda spooky out here, isn't it?"

"It's more like a dead zone. No animals running around or birds chirping. Nothing. Nothing but this piece of land, surrounded by trees as far as the eyes can see."

"What happened to the animals, anyway?"

"Rachel said that when she found her dad, all the animals were running loose. The pigs were out of their pen, the chicken coup door was opened and chickens were all over the place. The cows were still in the barn, but their stall doors were open. Animal Control came out and rounded them up and took them wherever you take abandoned farm animals."

"Wasn't there a dog?"

"There were two. But, when the cops got here, both were missing. No one knows where they ran off to and, as far as I know, neither one has been seen since."

"They ate the body and stuff, didn't they?" Peter asked.

"No one is sure. It could have been the dogs, but it could have been some wild animals, like foxes. Hell, it could have been pigs. Pigs have been known to devour an entire body. The bite marks on that leg they found didn't match a dog's bite. I'm guessing it was a pig that chewed on that leg bone."

"Too bad whoever killed Willerton wasn't smart enough to throw his body into the pigpen and let the pigs finish the job," Fisher said, laughing.

"You may find this funny, Peter, but I don't," Jessica said angrily.

"Sorry, that was out of line."

"It was. And, I'm sorry I snapped. It's just that this place is giving me the creeps. One thing I do know for sure, though."

"What's that?" Peter asked.

"Whoever killed Willerton must have really hated him to kill him the way he did. Obviously, they wanted the man to suffer."

"You're right about that."

Jessica glanced over at the barn. "Okay, then. Let's get started. We've got work to do."

Ninety minutes later Jessica and Peter were standing by the car, their investigation of the property completed.

"Ready, Peter?"

"Ready. Let's get out of here."

As Jessica turned to get into the car, she glanced over at a big old oak tree, about four hundred feet away, and noticed that it was fenced.

"Wait a minute. I want to see something," she told Peter. "I'll be right back."

"Where are you going?"

"I think that's a family cemetery on that little hill over there. I want to go take a look."

"What good will that do?"

"Family history, Peter. We didn't find a bible, but maybe those head markers will tell us something."

"That's a good idea. Let's go."

Jessica and Peter were quiet as they walked through the tall grass to the fence. As they approached it, Peter noticed a small gate to his right and opened it.

"After you," he said, gallantly and waved her through.

Jessica smiled. "It does take you back in time, doesn't it," she said.

"It does, indeed," Peter replied. "Well, let's see if

we can read any of these markers and find out who's been resting here for the past three hundred years."

"I don't think it's quite that long, Peter."

"Whatever. Hey, I can make this one out. It says Sarah Willerton."

"Is there a date?"

"No. It just has a name."

"Rachel told me that Sarah was Jack's mother's name. She ran off when Jack was a little boy," Jessica said. "This can't be the same woman, can it? If this is Jack's mother, how did she wind up here?"

"Maybe she came back."

"No, I don't think so. We need to find out if there was another Sarah Willerton."

"Here's a Mary Willerton," Peter told her, pointing to a head marker.

"That would be Jack Willerton's grandmother."

"I see. . . .." Peter was quiet as he counted the markers. "There are probably seven or eight more markers," Peter said. "I can't make out all of the names, though."

"I wonder who they are," Jessica said. "Some are lying on the ground, too. Damn! I wish we had found a bible or something."

"Do you want me to take pictures?"

"Please. Try to get some good shots of the head markers. Maybe, we'll be able to figure out who they belong to."

"Will do. And, then, let's get the hell out of here."

Chapter Ten

"You can't remember anything about your childhood?" Dr. Bentley asked Jessica.

"Nothing. At least, nothing before I was six or seven."

"That's highly unusual. Almost everyone has some memories of when they were little. I had a patient who remembered an incident that took place when she was only two."

"Well, I don't. However, I'm sure that the nightmares I'm having must have something to do with an event that happened when I was very young."

"Do the dreams ever differ?" Dr. Bentley asked.

"What happens may be different, but they always take place in a dark, scary forest and, at some point, my father is in them. Usually, I should say. He's usually in them. I've had a few nightmares where it's just me, but mostly he's in them."

"Do you remember your father?"

"Of course. He was a wonderful man. I loved him very much. I was devastated when my parents were killed," Jessica said, tears filling her eyes.

"How were your parents killed?" the doctor asked.

"A car accident. A couple of years ago. Same old story. A drunk ran them off the road and they hit a tree. They were killed instantly."

"I'm sorry to hear that."

"It still hurts to talk about it," Jessica said. "But they were wonderful parents and I have nothing but good memories of them. I can't remember that they ever spanked me, although I'm sure I deserved it more than once."

"However, you don't remember anything before you were six or seven," Dr. Bentley stated factually. "This is the period of your life that we are going to explore. This is where the secrets behind your nightmares lay. I'm sure of it."

"How can you be so sure," Jessica asked, starting to wonder if she had made a mistake coming here. She had barely told him anything about herself and he was already assuming that he knew what the problem was.

"Because it's my job to know."

Jessica got a puzzled look on her face. "That's it? That's not very reassuring, Doctor."

Dr. Jason Bentley smiled. "I'm sorry. I guess that was a little blunt. However, I'm going to ask you to trust me. I've been doing this for almost forty years. The only thing I'm going to ask from you is that you allow me to hypnotize you. There are things deep down in that brain of yours that have been suppressed for years. I want to get in there and take a look at what you're hiding – at what's causing these nightmares."

Jessica didn't say anything. The whole idea of being hypnotized scared her.

"You don't care for the idea, do you? I can tell just by the look on your face," Dr. Bentley said.

Jessica smiled. "I'm sorry, but you're right. I don't know what I'll say while I'm under and that bothers me."

"You need to be in control and the idea of giving that up, even if it's for a little while, scares you. I

64

understand, Jessica. But I'm not going to do anything that will harm you. We need to break through that wall you've built to protect yourself, and this is the only way I can do that."

"This is strictly between us, right? I mean, what if I did horrible things – are you going to tell anyone."

Dr. Bentley chuckled. "We're going back to when you were a little girl, Jessica. We're going to try to find memories of things that happened to you before you were six or seven years old. Things that you've been suppressing for years. I can't imagine that you did horrible things at such a young age. However, I do believe that something horrible happened to you, or something that you thought was horrible."

"I'll have to think about this."

"It's your choice, Jessica. However, if you don't do this, it is going to get worse. You know that. You already mentioned that the nightmares are more frequent and more terrifying."

"They are. I'd give anything to get a good night's sleep."

"As I said, the choice is yours. If you need time to think about it, that's fine. Give me a call if you decide to pursue this."

Jessica sighed, then looked over at Dr. Bentley and smiled. "I'll do it. I've nothing to lose and, if this works, everything to gain. When do we start?"

Dr. Bentley nodded his head in approval. "How about right now?"

Jessica looked surprised. "Right now?"

"No time like the present. So, let's get comfortable. Would you mind moving to the couch?"

Jessica glanced over at the couch. "You want me to lie down on the couch?"

"Please. This will work better for both of us if you are lying down."

"Do I have to take my shoes off?"

Dr. Bentley laughed. "No, Jessica. You can leave your shoes on."

"Are you going to record this?" Jessica asked.

"I am. Why do you ask?"

"I'd like to hear the recordings," she responded.

"That isn't necessary," Dr. Bentley said.

"Then, how will I know what I said?"

"I'll let you know if there are any breakthroughs.

Jessica considered his answer and shook her head no. "I want to hear the tapes," she emphatically stated.

"That might not be a good idea. It could be extremely disturbing to you. I'm not sure you are capable of handling it at this time."

"I'll handle it just fine. I'll only agree to this if you allow me to hear the recordings afterward."

Dr. Bentley turned his head and looked out of his office window, contemplating Jessica's ultimatum.

"Is that final?" he asked her.

"I need to know what I said. I need to hear it."

He smiled. "Then, hear it you shall. However, Jessica, don't forget that I warned you that this is not a good idea."

Jessica laughed. "Doc, I've spent a good deal of my life doing things that weren't good ideas. I think I'll be able to handle this."

"Well, I guess we'll find out, won't we?"

Dr. Bentley waited while Jessica made herself comfortable on the couch, wondering what secrets were hidden in that pretty little head.

Dr. Jason Bentley snapped his fingers. Jessica's head jerked up, she opened her eyes, saw Dr. Bentley with a huge grin on his face, and frowned.

"I don't know what you're so happy about. I'm done with this nonsense. It's obvious that it's not working," she told him. "I'm not going to waste money on this. I guess I'm one of those people that can't be hypnotized."

"You did it, Jessica. You regressed to six years old. You talked about your parents and a baby brother. I thought you were an only child, but you talked about a brother."

Jessica stared at him, confusion showing on her face. "I was under?"

"You certainly were. For about ten or fifteen minutes. I felt that was long enough for your first time."

"I want to hear the recording."

"We don't have time today. But, Jessica," Dr. Bentley said, excited, "you went to a deep level. This is extremely rare for the first time. You even sounded like a little girl."

"That's all well and good, Dr. Bentley, but it sounds made up. Why would I talk about a brother I never had? I was an only child."

"You cried out for him."

"Let me hear the recording," Jessica demanded.

"I will. However, I want to gather more

information first. Let me put you under a few more times and, then, we will listen to all of them at the same time. Fair?"

Jessica gave him a dirty look. "No, it's not fair. I only agreed to be hypnotized because you said I could listen to the recordings."

"And, you shall. Please, trust me on this. You're going to have questions after you listen to each recording. By being able to immediately listen to the next tape, you will probably get a lot of your questions answered. I know you're anxious to get to the bottom of your nightmares, but this is the best way to go."

Jessica didn't say anything. She turned her face away, not wanting the doctor to see that she was on the brink of crying.

"Jessica, please don't be upset. You've just taken the first step in getting to the root of your problems. This is huge. You should be celebrating that we're finally going to find out what is causing your dreams." He hesitated and said, "Although, I can't guarantee that what we find is going to be pretty. You know that, don't you?"

Jessica looked at him. "I know. But it can't be much worse than my nightmares." She gave him a little smile. "Or, can it?"

"I doubt it very much. Things that happen to us as children are often blown way out of proportion. We might find out that some simple little thing, such as losing a doll that you loved, is causing this."

"Or, watching a doll that I loved being torn to pieces by a dog, while my father watched and laughed at me for crying?"

Dr. Bentley stared at her. "Did that happen to you?"

"No. At least, I don't think so. But I didn't think I had a brother, either. So, I guess anything's possible."

"Where's all the anger coming from, Jessica?"

Jessica met his gaze and then looked away. "I'm sorry. I'm not angry. I'm just tired. I haven't had a good night's sleep in a long time."

"Doesn't that make you angry?"

"I guess it could. A little anyway."

"You guess?" Dr. Bentley asked her.

Jessica grinned. "Actually, it does. It really pisses me off."

Chapter Eleven

Jessica looked at the clock on her office wall. "What the hell," she muttered, wondering where the time had gone. Suddenly, it dawned on her that she had fallen asleep at her desk. It was almost ten o'clock and she was due in court in thirty minutes.

"Son of a bitch," she exclaimed, as she grabbed her jacket and briefcase and headed out the door. She figured she'd be late and Judge Finley would be pissed. Finley had a reputation for taking revenge on attorneys who messed up. He had a grudge against her and she figured every ruling he made today definitely would not be in her favor.

Jessica entered Judge Douglas Finley's courtroom just as Finley was taking his seat. He glanced up at her, watched her walk to the long table where the defense team sat, and frowned at her. "Well, well, Ms. Patterson. It's so nice you could join us today."

"Sorry, Judge." She smiled at him and took her seat next to Peter Fisher and Rachel Willerton.

"I understand your asking for another continuance," Judge Finley stated. "Why?"

Peter Fisher stood and faced him. "We need more time to examine new evidence that has just been given to us by the District Attorney."

Judge Finley looked over at the D.A. "Am I to understand that you held back evidence?"

The District Attorney stood and smiled. "Of course not, Your Honor. This evidence is new to us also, and we shared it with Mr. Fisher and Ms.

Patterson on a timely basis."

"What exactly are you referring to? What type of new evidence?"

"We believe that Ms. Willerton did not act alone when she committed the horrendous act of murdering her father and that she had an accomplice. We have just come across proof that she was involved with a young man and we have just started looking for him. We need time to talk to him and gather all the facts before we proceed. Actually, Judge, I was going to ask you for a continuance, but the defense beat me to it."

"Your Honor, this is ridiculous. Ms. Willerton did not kill her father nor did she play a part in his death. The very assumption that she was involved in this crime is ludicrous," stated Peter Fisher.

"I believe that is for a jury to decide, Mr. Fisher." The judge looked at Jessica. "What about you, Ms. Patterson?"

Jessica looked up at him. "Excuse me? What about me?"

"Are you talking to me, Ms. Patterson? Because, I sure don't see you standing."

Jessica rose and stared at him. "Sorry. What about me, Your Honor?"

"Do you have anything to add?" he asked.

"No, Your Honor."

"Request denied," Judge Finley stated. "Next case."

"But, Your Honor . . ." Fisher stammered, before Judge Finley interrupted him.

"You're done here, Mr. Fisher. I've ruled. Now leave. I've got more to deal with this morning than you and your foolish requests."

"Your Honor?" said the D.A.

"What is it?"

"I'll be submitting a request for a continuance later today. We do need a little more time."

Judge Finley stared at him. "Fine. Submit it. I'll give you another week. But, that's it. Understand?"

"Yes, Your Honor. Thank you."

"Now, get the hell out of my courtroom. All of you."

Ten minutes later they were sitting at a table in one of the conference rooms outside of the courtroom. Rachel glanced at Jessica, with a confused look on her face. "What was that all about?" she asked.

Jessica sighed. "The District Attorney thinks that you and Ted Williams killed your father."

"Ted Williams? I barely know him. He was a couple of years ahead of me in high school. I think he was a senior when I was a freshman."

"How well do you really know him, Rachel?"

"I just told you that I barely know him. I mean, I know who he is and all, but he's not a friend or anything."

"Did you ever date?"

Rachel looked surprised. "Date? Of course, not."

"So, Rachel, if we ask around school and talk to your friends, are they going to tell us that you hardly knew him and you weren't a couple?"

"I guess."

"What do you mean, you guess?"

"I mean, that's what they should say. But, how

am I supposed to know what they'll say? All I can tell you is that I certainly didn't kill my father and this Ted guy certainly didn't help me."

Jessica looked at Peter. "What do you think, Peter? Do you believe her?"

Peter stared at Rachel and said, "How could I not believe that innocent little face?"

Rachel smiled. "See? Peter believes me."

"Do you, Peter? Do you believe her?"

"You know what I believe, Jessica?" Peter asked.

"What's that?"

Jessica waited while Peter reached into his briefcase and pulled out a folder. He opened it and took out two photos and handed them to Jessica. "This is what I believe."

Jessica looked at the photos, then, laid them in front of Rachel. "We got these from the District Attorney, Rachel."

Rachel stared at the photos, then, looked up at Jessica and Peter and shrugged. "So?"

Jessica sat back in her chair and fixed eyes with Rachel. "Are you saying you don't know who these people are?"

"Not for positive sure. The guy looks a little like Ted Williams. But I haven't seen him in years, so I can't be sure."

"Unfuckingbelievable," Jessica exclaimed. "How can you look at a picture of yourself and not know it's you? Are you that dense?"

"Don't call me dense. That's not me," Rachel replied, her voice shaking. "I admit it looks a little like me, but that certainly is not me in that picture. It looks like my . . ."

"Do you have a twin?" Jessica interrupted, practically yelling at her. "Because, unless you have an identical twin, the District Attorney is going to say that is you, screwing Ted Williams."

"Yes, okay?" Rachel said, raising her voice.

"Yes, what?"

"I kinda have a twin. She's not exactly my twin. She's my cousin, but we look a lot alike. We used to joke that we could be twins. Her name is Jillian Wickstrom. Her mom and my mom are sisters. That could be her in those pictures."

Peter fell back in his chair, his mouth open. "Holy shit. It looks like the D.A. is in for a big surprise."

"You think?" replied Jessica. "Their whole case is based on the fact that Rachel had help when she murdered her father, and they think these pictures will prove that it was the Williams boy. They think this is Rachel and her big, strong boyfriend who helped her murder and cut up her father

Peter chuckled. "I can't wait to see the look on the D.A.'s face when we bring Jillian Wickstrom to the stand."

"You won't be able to do that," Rachel said.

"Why not?" Peter asked.

"Because, Jillian is missing. She's been missing for weeks."

"Peter," Jessica asked, "where did the cops find these pictures?"

"I believe they found them in the barn. There were some boxes buried under some hay up in the loft.

These pictures were in one of those boxes."

"What else did they find?" Jessica inquired.

"A few more pictures, like these. Basically, porn. Most of them were of young girls. I mean, really young."

"That makes sense. After all, he started molesting Rachel when she was only ten. Were any of those pictures, that they found in the barn, of Rachel?"

"Nope," Peter told her.

She turned to Rachel and asked, "Did you see a lot of your cousin when you were young?"

"She and my aunt visited a lot while my mom was still around. After my mom left, I hardly saw Jillian. She visited a couple of times, but I probably haven't seen her in four years or so."

"How old would she be now?" Jessica asked.

Rachel thought for a second. "Nineteen or twenty. She's three and a half years older than me."

"She would have been fifteen the last time Rachel saw her," Peter said. "Age is about right. Willerton liked them young."

"Rachel, did you ever see your dad fooling around with Jillian?"

"Not really. I remember one time, though, when she came running into the house crying. She left right after that."

"She drove?" asked Peter. "You said she was fifteen when you last saw her. That's too young to have a license to drive. Are you sure about the age?"

"I'm sure, and she wasn't driving yet. She made a call and a little while later this car showed up and she left. It was the last time I saw her."

"Was it Ted who picked her up?"

Rachel shrugged. "I don't know. I guess it could have been. The two of them did come out to the farm a few times. I guess that's when my dad took that picture. He must have seen them messing around in the barn or something."

Jessica stood up and started pacing back and forth. "Peter, we've got to find that girl, and the sooner the better."

"And, her boyfriend, Ted Williams," Peter responded.

"She's a woman now. If what we suspect happened – that Willerton raped her - is true, it could be she finally decided to get revenge."

"Well," Peter replied, "if that's what happened, she did one hell of a job."

Chapter Twelve

Dr. Bentley slowly brought Jessica back to the present. She had been under for almost an hour, and as much as he would have liked to continue, he knew he had exceeded the time limit. Plus, he had another patient in the waiting room, who expected to be seen on time.

"You did well, Jessica."

"Have I filled in more pieces of the puzzle?" she asked.

"Definitely. We made a lot of progress today."

"Can I listen to the tape?" Jessica inquired.

"Sorry, we're out of time, but I want to go over this with you as soon as possible. Are you busy tonight?"

Jessica looked surprised. "You want me to come back tonight?"

"If you can. I'd like you to hear it today, if at all possible. I don't want to wait until your next appointment."

"I'll be here. What time?"

"How about eight? Wait a minute." He glanced down at his appointment book. "Nine is better for me. Can you be here at nine?"

Jessica smiled. "Nine it is, Dr. Bentley. I can hardly wait."

Four hours and forty-five minutes later, Jessica was seated in Dr. Bentley's office, softly crying.

"I'm so sorry, Doctor. It's just that this is. . ." She hesitated, looking for the right words. "I can't believe . . ." She looked over at him.

"Don't even try to put it into words, Jessica. This is strange, I'll admit. But I have to believe that there's some truth to it. Your subconscious mind didn't make that all up."

"But I talked about a brother. That's got to be a mistake. And, if that's not right, then how can anything else be true? It's just a bunch of mumbo jumbo."

"Did you ever know a Carl? Perhaps, you had a relative or a cousin named that."

"Dr. Bentley, I just listened to a little girl talk about her brother. It couldn't be me. I was an only child. This is ridiculous."

"Think about it, Jessica. Your nightmares are always about being lost in a dark, scary forest. You previously told me that, in some of them, you see your father carrying a bundle, which could be a baby. Plus, Jessica, you did mention Carl once before."

"When? I don't remember hearing a tape with that name in it."

"It was one of the first sessions. In it, you mention that you and Carl are sleeping in the woods and when you wake up, he's gone."

"I said the name Carl? I don't remember saying a name. I remember when I listened to that tape, I said my brother – not his name."

"You might be right. Perhaps it was on a different tape. The name rings a bell, though. At some point, I'm sure you mentioned Carl."

Jessica was quiet, thinking about what Dr. Bentley had said. She looked over at him, then, quickly looked away. "Oh, my god," she uttered. "No, it can't be true," she cried out.

"What is it? You remembered something, didn't you?"

"I killed him," she exclaimed. "I killed my baby brother."

"Jessica, look at me," Dr. Bentley told her.

Jessica stood, grabbed her purse, and started walking towards the door. "I've got to leave now."

"No!" Dr. Bentley yelled. "You're not leaving, yet. Sorry, I didn't mean to shout at you. But you can't leave yet. You've just had a memory and we need to pursue this right now. You've got to tell me why you think you killed Carl."

Jessica shook her head no. "I can't. I don't want to talk about it."

"Jessica," Dr. Bentley said, quietly. "I want you to sit down and relax. Would you like a cup of coffee?"

Jessica looked over at him. "Do you have anything stronger?"

Dr. Bentley smiled. "Whiskey or Scotch?"

"Whiskey, please. Straight up."

Dr. Bentley poured a few fingers of whiskey into a glass and handed it to her.

"Thank you," Jessica said, as she took a sip. "Aren't you joining me?"

"Not tonight. Please, sit down." He waited while Jessica made herself comfortable. "Now – very slowly – I want you to tell me what you just remembered. Sit back and close your eyes, if that helps."

Jessica sat back and took another swallow of her drink. "This is hard."

"I know."

"It's just that it's confusing to me. Everything is all jumbled up in my head," she said.

"What did you remember?" Dr. Bentley asked again.

Jessica sighed. "I'm little. Maybe five or six years old. I'm wearing a pair of pants and a sweater. A blue sweater. It's my favorite color." Jessica stopped talking and looked over at the doctor. "It's still my favorite color," she said.

"Let's not dwell on the sweater. What else do you remember?"

"We're in a room. It's a big room, and a woman is on the floor."

"What's she doing on the floor?" Dr. Bentley asked, interrupting her.

"She's just lying there. She's not moving."

"Where is your brother?"

"He's on a couch. He's crying really hard. I have to stop him from crying. The man is going to hit him if he doesn't stop crying. He's yelling at me to shut him up or else."

"What did you do?"

"I patted him on his back and told him to be quiet, but he wouldn't stop crying. I put a pillow over his face, so the man couldn't hear him crying anymore."

"Do you know who the man is, Jessica?"

"I think he's my father, but that can't be right. My father doesn't look like that."

"What does the woman look like?"

"I don't know." Jessica started breathing hard.

80

"My mother and father don't look like these people. I don't understand," she said, tears rolling down her cheeks.

"Look at me," Dr. Bentley said.

Jessica glanced over at him; a questioning look on her face.

"Jessica," Dr. Bentley said. "Take a couple of deep breaths."

She glanced at him, then, took another swallow of her drink. "This works better," she said.

Dr. Bentley nodded in agreement. "It sometimes does. I think we're done for tonight. You've had a major breakthrough, Jessica. The fact that you remembered something about your childhood is extremely promising."

"But I only remembered after I listened to the tape. Perhaps, my mind is playing tricks with me."

"I don't think so. I think you saw your father hurt your mother, which is trauma enough to scar a child. The possibility also exists that you smothered your baby brother to keep him quiet. If that's the case, it was an accident and not your fault. You were trying to protect him so your father wouldn't hurt him. You were trying to help him, Jessica. Remember, it wasn't your fault."

"But, why didn't I remember this before now?"

"It's called a defense mechanism. For all these years, your brain has blocked it all out to protect you.

"So, why am I remembering now? What's changed?"

"Well, for one thing, you're seeing me because of your nightmares and we're dredging up things that you have hidden for years. It could be that. Or, it could be that something else triggered your memory. We may never know for sure. Whatever, it was, let's keep going. We still need to figure out why you're lost in a scary forest, don't we?"

"Do we? I wonder, now, if I really want to find out."

Chapter Thirteen

"I want to go back out to the Willerton farm," Jessica told Peter Fisher.

"What in hell for?"

"I have the feeling we missed something."

"Jessica, the cops have gone through that place with a fine-tooth comb. There's nothing left to find."

"You're probably right, Peter. It's just that I have this feeling that I should take another look. Don't worry. You don't have to go with me."

"It's not that I don't want to go with you. I just think it's a big waste of time."

"Maybe, but it's my time. By the way, are you done researching the Willerton family history?"

"I've gone as far as I can. There wasn't a whole lot of information at City Hall," Peter told her.

"See if you can find Jillian Wickstrom's mother. She might know a thing or two about that family."

"Do you know where she lives?" Peter inquired.

"No, but Rachel should know. You can ask her the next time you talk to her."

"I'm going over to juvie this afternoon. I'll ask her then."

"So, what did you find out about the Willerton family?"

"Like I said, not a whole lot. It does seem that the women in that family tended to run away. Or, just disappear."

"What are you trying to tell me?" Jessica asked.

Fisher reached into his briefcase and pulled out a file. He opened it and pulled out a stack of photos with sticky notes on them.

"These are the pictures I took at the cemetery," he told Jessica. He shuffled through them, putting them in order. "Okay, here we go," he said, as he looked at the first photo. "The grave markers that I could read on this one say Peter Willerton and Mary Willerton. Those would be Jack's father and grandmother."

"That's one wife that didn't run off," Jessica said.

"Maybe, she couldn't because Joshua Willerton killed her," Fisher remarked.

"You have no proof of that, so stop making stuff up," Jessica said, grinning.

"Right," Fisher said. "Next, we have a marker with the name of Simon on it. There's also a marker with the name of Sarah and the letters – W i l - on it. That would most likely be Willerton. According to Rachel, her grandmother ran away when Jack was just a little kid, so who is this Sarah? Did she come back to Jack and his father or is it a relative? The plot thickens."

"Do we need the commentaries? Go on."

"On this photo, I can make out the letters M r i W l and o."

Jessica gave Peter a strange look.

"What?" he asked.

"What was the name of Jack's first wife? Wasn't it Marie?" Jessica asked.

"Ya. Why?"

"Well, obviously, that name is Marie."

"Maybe, but it doesn't mean it's Jack's mother," Fisher said.

"Right. What's on the other pictures?"

"There's a Vincent. I can't make out all the letters of the last name, but it looks like it could also be Willerton. The date says April 6, 1980."

"When was Vincent born?" Jessica asked.

"Good question, but there's only that date."

"It could have been Jack's kid," Jessica stated. "Perhaps, a stillbirth. Maybe born and died the same day."

"There's no birth or death record at City Hall for a Vincent Willerton," Fisher said.

"Are there any more names that you can make out?"

"One more. It looks a little newer than the rest." Peter looked a little closer at the photo and frowned.

"What?" Jessica asked.

"It's a baby. Born in January 1990 and died six months later, in July 1990."

"Is there a name?"

"Yes, it's Carl. Carl Willerton."

Jessica grabbed the photo out of Peter's hand and stared at it. "What do you mean, Carl Willerton? How do you know what it says? I can't read that."

"Because I used a magnifying glass to read it."

"Give me the glass." Jessica reached out her hand, expecting Peter to put a magnifying glass in it.

"I don't have it with me, Jessica. Geez, what are you so upset about?"

"Are you sure this says Carl?"

"I'm positive. What's with you, anyway?"

Jessica reached for her water bottle and took a big drink.

"Are you okay?" Peter asked her.

"I'm fine. I'm sorry. I don't know what came over me." Jessica took another drink of water. She was quiet for a few seconds, breathed deeply, and asked, "Aren't there three or four more markers?"

"I think three. But I can't make out the names on those markers from the pictures. Jessica, obviously you're upset about something. You went white when I mentioned Carl Willerton's name. What's going on?"

"Nothing is going on, Peter. Just forget about it. Okay?"

"You don't want to talk about it?"

"Right. So, just drop it, will you?" Jessica replied.

Peter started to answer, then thought better of it. "Are you still going to drive out to the Willerton farm this weekend?" Peter asked her, changing the subject.

"I plan on going out early tomorrow."

"I'm coming with you," Peter stated.

"That's not necessary."

"I didn't ask, Jessica. I'm telling you that I'm coming with you. What time are we leaving in the morning?"

Jessica looked at him and smiled. "Thanks, Peter. How about seven?"

"Works for me. I'll see you then," Peter replied.

"Bye," Jessica said and headed towards the door. She turned and watched Peter, as he started putting the pictures back into the folder.

Peter looked up at her. "Is there something else?"

"Do you have any shovels?"

86

"Shovels? Sorry, I don't. I live in an apartment. I've never had a need for a shovel."

"Will you stop at a hardware store tonight and pick up a couple? You know, the digging kind – not the snow shoveling kind."

"We're going to dig?"

"We just might. It's best to be prepared. See ya." She gave a little wave goodbye and left the room, closing the door behind her.

Chapter Fourteen

"We could get into deep shit trouble for this," Peter said. He reached into the back pocket of his pants, pulled out a hanky, and wiped the sweat off of his forehead.

"Just dig, will you?" Jessica answered. "We should be deep enough pretty soon, don't you think?"

"We? I don't see you with a shovel in your hands," Peter muttered. "Why are we digging him up, anyway?"

"I need to know that there's really a body buried there."

"Of course, there's a body here. There was a grave marker, wasn't there? See, it's right there!" Peter practically shouted as he pointed to the wood marker that was resting against the fence.

"I need to see the coffin."

Peter pushed the shovel deep into the hole, bringing out another shovelful of dirt.

"Did you hear that?" Jessica cried out.

"What?"

"It sounded like you hit something."

Peter took the shovel and pushed the tip of it down into the hole, striking wood. "You're right. This is it. Now, can I stop digging and fill this hole back up? This isn't right, messing with the dead like this."

"Uncover it."

"Come on, Jessica. You wanted to be sure that there was a coffin buried here and there is. What in hell do I need to uncover the whole thing for?"

"Please, Peter, just do it."

"Not until you tell me what's going on." Peter threw down the shovel and stared at her.

Jessica walked over to the small cemetery's fence and slowly turned, taking in the landscape that surrounded the farm. For three to four hundred yards, in each direction, there was flat open land. But, once past the land that had been cleared, as far as the eyes could see, the property was surrounded by trees. She shuddered, feeling a cold chill run through her body.

"Jessica!"

She turned, startled by the sound.

"Jessica, are you all right?"

She looked confused for a second, then, smiled, giving her head a little shake. "Peter," she stated.

"What the fuck, Jessica?"

"Sorry. I don't know what came over me. It's this place, I guess. Somehow, I feel connected to it. It's like I've been here before."

"You were. A few weeks ago, with me. Remember? Now, can we get out of here?" Peter asked.

"Oh, we can't go yet. I still need to see what's inside of that coffin."

Peter stared at her. "Are you kidding me? You said you wanted to see if there was a coffin. Well, there is. Now, you want to see if there's a body in there? Go ahead and look. You crawl down there and open that coffin because I'm sure as hell not doing it."

Without a word, Jessica walked over to the opening, picked up the shovel, and proceeded to remove the rest of the dirt that was on top of the coffin. As Peter watched her, he started to feel guilty and walked over to the grave. He reached down for her hand. "Get out of there," he said.

"I don't need your help," Jessica snapped at him.

"Take my hand. I'll open it for you."

Jessica hesitated, then, reached up and took Peter's hand. "It's small, Peter. The coffin is really small."

Peter didn't say anything as he finished removing the dirt that was still on top of the coffin. Using the edge of the shovel, he pried open the lid just enough to peek inside. "No way," he uttered as he glanced up at Jessica with a surprised look on his face.

"It's empty. There's no friggin' body," he cried out. Jessica's face didn't register surprise and he suddenly realized that she knew the grave would be empty. "You knew it would be empty, didn't you?"

"Not for sure. But I figured it might be."

"How did you know?"

Jessica shook her head. "I just knew. Now, let's go see if we can make out what those other three markers say."

"In a minute. I need to fill the grave back up. We can't leave it like this," Peter said.

"Go ahead," she mumbled, as she walked over to look at the markers that weren't legible on the photos. As she walked away from Peter, Jessica noticed a small cross lying in the grass. She bent down and turned it over to read it

"Shit," she exclaimed.

"What's the matter," Peter asked her.

"It's another child. The dates are 1984 to 1990."

"Can you make out the name?" Peter asked her.

"Just a couple of letters. It looks like the first one is C. I can make out an r and an e. The last name is probably Willerton. I can see an o and n at the end."

"Well, if it is a Willerton, it was probably another one of Jack's kids."

Jessica laid the cross back in the grass. "You're probably right. I wonder how many kids he actually had from his first marriage."

"I found birth records for two, but no deaths were ever recorded.

Jessica sighed. "I figure we'll never know for sure." She looked over at Peter, who was still shoveling the dirt back into the hole. "I'm sorry, Peter."

He glanced over at her and smiled. "For what? Why are you sorry?"

"For bringing you out here. It was a wild goose chase."

"How can you say that? We found out that there's a body missing from a coffin. I mean, that's big news."

"Ya, right. News that we can't tell anyone about. However, what I meant was that I'm sorry we didn't find anything to help Rachel."

"Oh, right. That's a bummer. But, shouldn't we report this missing body to someone?"

"And, get into trouble because we dug up a grave without approval? I don't think so."

"We could say that Rachel gave us her permission. After all, she's the only surviving child. This place is hers now."

"I don't think that would fly."

"So, tell me. How did you really know that there

was no body in that grave?"

Jessica smiled and shook her head. "Not today. Maybe, someday I'll tell you, but not today

.

Chapter Fifteen

"Let's walk for a while before we leave," Jessica said.

"What the hell for?" Peter asked. "You said this place gives you the creeps. Hell, it gives me the creeps."

"I'm not ready to leave, yet. You can go sit in the car if you want. I want to check out the barn one more time. And, maybe look at the house to see if we missed anything."

"Jessica, wait," Peter called out, as she started to walk away from the cemetery towards the house.

Jessica turned and looked at him. "What?"

"Wait for me. I'll join you. I want to put the shovels back in the car first."

Jessica smiled at him. "Well, hurry up. I want to be out of this place before dark."

"We've got a lot of time before it'll be dark. It's only. . ." Peter glanced at his watch. "It's almost six-thirty. Where the hell did the time go?" he exclaimed.

"You know what they say, don't you? Time sure flies when . . .."

"I know. When you're having fun," Peter added, finishing the sentence for her. "We sure proved that old saying wrong, as I sure as hell didn't have any fun today. Unless you consider digging up coffins fun, which I don't."

"Sorry, but I didn't know we drove out here to have fun. Just, hurry up, will you? I'll meet you at the house," Jessica said and continued walking down the hill.

"I can't believe it," Peter said.

"Really, Peter. That's about the tenth time you've said that. Please, believe it."

"But, look what we found. I don't get how the cops and the CSI and everybody else missed it?"

"Well, we missed it, too, the first time we were here."

"But we were just checking the place out when we were here before. I can't believe we found this stuff. Do you think this will help her?" Peter asked.

Jessica took her eyes off the road long enough to glance over at Peter. He grinned at her. He looks like a kid in a candy shop and someone just gave him twenty bucks and told him to go crazy, she thought.

"Are you serious?" Jessica replied. "We just found his stash hidden under a floorboard. My God, Peter, with this evidence there's not a jury in the world that will convict her. These pictures show her being molested by her father. That sick son of a bitch raped her. He forced her to perform oral sex on him, and he photographed it, for crying out loud. If he wasn't already dead, I'd kill the bastard myself."

"She looks really young in some of those pictures," Peter commented.

"Remember, she said, "he started molesting her when she was around ten years old."

"It looks like he took pictures from the very beginning," Peter said. "How can a man do that to his daughter? I can't begin to imagine what kind of a sick fuck can do that."

"I wonder why Rachel never mentioned the pictures. She must have known he was taking them."

"I guess," Peter agreed. "But, remember, she also said she enjoyed having sex with her father."

"That's true," Jessica agreed. "That is one part of her story we need to keep to ourselves. If she ever admitted that to anyone else and it got out, the jury would turn on her in a minute."

"I wonder why he hid the family bible. That doesn't make sense. What could there be in there that he didn't want anyone to see?"

"Where'd you put it?" Jessica asked him.

"The Bible?" Peter asked.

"Yes. Where is it?"

"It's in the back seat, in my briefcase."

"Can you reach it?"

"Sure. Why?"

"We've got about an hour before we'll be back in Iron Mountain. How about you read it to me?"

Peter gave her a puzzling look. "You want me to read the bible to you?"

Jessica smiled. "No, not the bible. I want you to read what's written in the front of the bible. The Willerton family history."

"Oh, sorry," Peter said. "Of course. The family history." He removed his seatbelt and reached into the back of the car, and retrieved his case. He took out the bible and opened the cover.

"Your seatbelt," Jessica said.

"What?"

"Fasten your seatbelt."

"Right," Peter put his seatbelt back on, opened

95

the cover of the book, and started reading.

"The first entry is for a Joshua Willerton, born May 10, 1866. That's probably Jack's grandfather," Peter said, looking over at Jessica.

"If it is, then, that entry was made by one of Jack's great-grandparents."

"How do you know that?" Peter asked.

"Obviously, it had to be a parent that wrote it. Or, at least a close relative or a friend of Joshua's family."

"Right. But, don't you think that whoever it was, it had to be a Willerton and not a friend? After all, this is their family bible."

"I would think so," Jessica replied, agreeing with Peter.

"Look at this, Jessica," Peter said, turning the book so she could see the writing. "The penmanship is spectacular. It's all flowery looking and easy to read. I'm surprised. I didn't think many of the settlers knew how to read or write."

Jessica glanced over at him, then, looked back to concentrate on her driving. "I'll look later when I'm not driving a car, if you don't mind."

"Sorry," Peter told her.

"It makes perfect sense that they knew how to read and write. Remember, quite a few of the settlers were educated people who left the big cities in the east to find a new life. They were enticed by promises of hundreds of acres of land to settle on and an exciting new life. Many of them sold everything they had to move west. When they realized that what they were actually going to get was a life of hardship and sorrow, it was too late to turn back. At least, it was for most of them. Some of those pioneers realized, early on, that they had bit off more than they could chew and turned around and went back to the homes they had left. Those were the lucky ones. The ones who still had a home to go back to or hadn't spent all their money preparing for the trip west."

"I can't imagine doing what those people did - moving into strange, unchartered territory," Peter commented. He looked out the window and noted a road sign indicating that it was forty miles to Iron Mountain. "We've still got a way to go," he informed Jessica.

"I know. I saw the sign. So, what else does the good book tell us?" Jessica asked, smiling.

"The next entry is for Rebecca Willerton."

"What does it say," Jessica inquired.

"She died on April 2, 1886. And, Seth Willerton died two years later on April 2, 1888."

"Oh, my god," Jessica said. "They died on the same date, two years apart."

"Looks like it."

"So, if those are Joshua's parents, he would have been around twenty years old when they died."

"And, he probably took over the farm. A lot of work for a young kid," Peter stated.

"In today's standards, that's young. But, back in those days, kids grew up fast. The parents put them to work on the farm when they were only five and six years old. Everyone had to pull their weight. Does it look like he had any brothers or sisters?"

Peter scanned down the page in the bible. "There

aren't any entries showing any other children being born to Rebecca and Seth. If they had any kids besides Joshua, they aren't recorded in this bible."

"What's next?" Jessica asked.

"Looks like Joshua found himself a wife. He married Mary Samuels on October 29, 1903." Peter thought for a second before he added, "He was thirty-seven years old. He waited a long time to marry."

"It stands to reason that there may not have been a whole lot of single women to choose from, back then. I wonder how old she was when she married him," Jessica responded.

"This is rather a long history of the Willertons, Jessica. I'd like to chart it out – you know, like a family tree. Maybe, we can make better sense out of it that way."

"You're probably right. We're just guessing about Rebecca and Seth Willerton, assuming they are Rachel's great-great-grandparents."

"It is interesting, though. Do you think all of these people are buried in that cemetery?"

"No. We know they aren't all buried there. We didn't find a body in Carl's so-called grave, did we? I wonder how many more of those graves are empty. I wonder how many other poor souls are out there - suffering and waiting for their bodies to be found so they can finally be properly put to rest."

"Maybe Carl isn't even dead," Peter mused.

Jessica turned her head and stared at him. "What do you mean, isn't even dead?"

Peter shrugged. "Sorry, I was just thinking out loud. Never mind me."

"Although, why would someone bury an empty coffin? It doesn't make a lot of sense, does it?"

"Not really. What if all of the graves are empty, Jessica? What if grave robbers snuck in during the middle of the night and took all the bodies?"

"I think you've watched too many horror movies, Peter, and your imagination is running wild."

Peter laughed. "Is it? Well, I guess we'll never know, will we? Unless, of course, we dig up all those graves."

Chapter Sixteen

"Forget it!" Rachel yelled. "I'm not pleading guilty to something I didn't do."

Jessica watched as Rachel paced back and forth between the door and the window that overlooked Charles Street. She had been crying, her face was red, and snot was running out of her nose onto her upper lip. Jessica reached into her purse and pulled out a couple of tissues and handed them to Rachel.

"Wipe your nose," she demanded.

Peter looked at Jessica and shrugged. "We can't make her, you know. If she doesn't want to plead guilty by reason of temporary insanity, then we can't make her."

"I know that, Peter," Jessica snapped back at him. "But we've got to make her understand that this is her best chance of not spending the rest of her life in prison."

"I'd rather spend my life in jail than admit to something I didn't do," Rachel yelled. "Just because you found some dirty pictures doesn't mean I suddenly went nuts and killed my father."

"Rachel, listen to me. If we go to trial with a temporary insanity plea and the jury sees these pictures and what your father did to you for the past six years, they aren't going to convict you. They'll understand that you reached a point where you couldn't take any more of his abuse, went crazy for a little while, and retaliated."

Rachel blew her nose again and sat down at the

table next to Peter. "Peter, do you agree with Jessica? Can you guarantee me 100% that I'll get off? Can you promise me that, Peter? Because, if you say you can, you're a fucking liar. You don't know what a jury is going to do. They're unpredictable. My god, I'm just a kid and I know that much."

Jessica pulled some papers out of her briefcase and laid them on the table in front of her.

"What are those?" Rachel asked her.

"Just some notes."

"About what?" Rachel inquired.

"Your family history," Jessica said.

"What does that have to do with anything?"

"Did your father ever talk about your mother and where she is?" Jessica asked her.

"No. He hated her for running off and leaving him with a kid. I have no idea where she is. Hell, for all I know, she's dead."

"I don't think so," said Jessica. "We couldn't find any death records for her. It would be a great help if we could talk to her."

"I don't get it," Rachel said. "She ran off six years ago. What would she know about anything?"

"Rachel, there had to be a reason that she left you and your father. It's not unusual for a wife to run away from her husband, but it is unusual for a mother to leave her kids behind. It might help your case if we could find out what went on in that house - if we could understand what was so horrible that she abandoned you."

Rachel stood up, knocking her chair over, and started pacing the room again. "Do you want to know why she left? I'll tell you why! She left because she was a selfish bitch who didn't give a shit about me. That's all there's to it. It's no big mystery. She left me behind to be fucked day in and day out by that bastard. She didn't care about. . .."

Rachel turned away from Jessica and Peter as she started sobbing. Her body trembled as she dropped to her knees, held her face in her hands, and wept. Jessica went over to her, bent down, put her arms around her, and held her.

"You poor, little girl," Jessica said. "You poor, poor little girl."

Peter watched as Jessica comforted Rachel. He suddenly grinned and said, "We just won our case, Jessica. If Rachel can repeat that performance in court, there isn't a jury in this world that will convict her."

Jessica looked up at him, a surprised look on her face. "What did you just say?"

"If Rachel can repeat what she just said to a jury, with the same emotion that I just witnessed, she'll get off scot-free. All we need to do is make sure we have women on the jury who have daughters, who can relate."

"But that means putting her on the stand, Peter," Jessica replied. "You know that's not a good idea. It's never a good idea to put the defendant on the stand, especially in a murder trial."

"Look at her," Peter said. "Take a good look."

Jessica stood and walked a few feet away from Rachel and looked down at her. Rachel looked up at Jessica and Jessica realized Peter was right.

"She looks like an innocent, little girl who is in pain. God, Peter, it breaks my heart just to look at her like this - all broken into pieces."

"What do you think?" Peter asked.

"I think you may be right. It might just work."

Rachel looked confused as she listened to the conversation. "What are you talking about?"

Jessica smiled and reached out her hand to her. "Get up off that floor. We need to talk and you need to listen."

Still confused, Rachel took Jessica's hand and stood up. "What's going on?" she asked.

"Sit down, Rachel," Peter said. "We've got a lot to go through in the next hour."

"Like what?" Rachel asked.

"Well, first of all, you have to quit smiling and being so friendly to everyone. You have to show everyone how depressed you are, Rachel. You have to be withdrawn and sad all the time. You've gone through horrible things and it's affected you deeply. When you break down on the stand, it has to be real. We need the jury to sympathize with you," Peter told her.

Jessica shook her head in agreement. "We need to establish that this is normal for you and that you're not a happy, carefree teenager. It shouldn't be that hard to play the part. Anyone, who has experienced what you have, would be depressed – almost suicidal," she explained to Rachel.

"I'm not saying I was nuts."

"Don't worry. You won't have to say it," Peter told her.

"So, what you're saying, if I got it right, is that I'm so upset for my mother leaving me and my father fucking me that I'm ready to kill myself. Is that right?"

"Exactly," Peter replied.

Rachel thought for a second and then smiled.

"What?" Jessica asked. "Why are you so happy? Didn't you just hear what we told you about not being so damned happy?"

"Of course, I heard you. But, wouldn't it be even better if I actually did try to kill myself?"

Chapter Seventeen

"I just want to talk today."

Dr. Bentley took the end of his pen and scratched his left ear. "I see," he mumbled. He continued scratching for a couple more seconds and, then, looked over at Jessica. "Is there anything, in particular, you want to discuss?"

Jessica watched him put the pen back on his desk. She glanced at it and then at him. "Do you have a problem with your ear? Because, if you had scratched any harder it would be bleeding."

Dr. Bentley shook his head no. "I'm fine. But my ears have been itchy all morning."

"So, you're not fine."

"I used a different shampoo this morning. There must be something in it that's making me itch." He smiled at her. "Sorry. I'm sure you didn't come here to listen to me complain about itchy ears. What is it you want to talk about?"

"I went back out to the Willerton farm this past weekend."

Dr. Bentley looked surprised. "Do you think that was a good idea?"

"I wasn't sure if it was at the time, but now I'm glad I did."

"You didn't go out there by yourself, did you?"

"No. Peter Fisher went with me."

"He's the attorney for that Willerton girl, isn't he? The one you're working with."

"He is," Jessica replied. "He's a pretty good guy. He's definitely a fast learner. He's doing a much better job than I anticipated he would."

"Exactly what was your motive for going out there again, Jessica?"

"There's a graveyard on a hill overlooking the farm. There are generations of Willertons buried there, going back to Rachel Willerton's great-great-grandfather, Seth Willerton. The first time Peter and I went to the farm, we checked it out. Quite a few of the grave markers are still standing. Some of them are lying in the grass, rotting away. I guess you could say they are all rotting away. Some just faster than others."

"What do you mean when you say grave markers, Jessica? Are you talking about headstones?"

Jessica shook her head. "No. Most of them are either wooden crosses or pieces of wood, with names and dates scratched into them. On some of them, you can still make out the writing. I call them grave markers because they aren't stone or granite and I don't know what else to call them."

"Grave marker is as good a name as any. Sometimes, they are called headboards, but grave marker is a correct term. But, how did you think this would help. . ." Dr. Bentley hesitated. "Rachel," he finally blurted out. "Sorry, I forgot her name for a minute."

"I didn't know if it would help her. But we did find a family bible hidden under some floorboards in the house, along with a box of disgusting pictures that Rachel's father took while he molested her."

"Won't that help her case?"

"Oh, it definitely will help her case," Jessica

responded. "Those pictures of her being abused by that rotten son of a bitch are definitely going to help. But the reason I wanted to go back was that the date, on one of the markers, indicated that a baby was buried there."

Dr. Bentley looked confused. "I don't understand why you would be interested in that. What are you getting at?"

"The marker was placed there to identify a grave for a baby named Carl."

Dr. Bentley frowned. "And, what was the last name on the marker, Jessica?" he asked, hesitantly.

"Willerton. We're quite sure the child's name was Carl Willerton. He was six months old when he died."

Dr. Bentley stared at her, shaking his head. "No, Jessica. I know what you're thinking, but you have to be wrong. There are a lot of Carls in this world, you know."

"The first time I was in that house, I felt ill. It was all too familiar – everything was. It was like I'd been there before. What about all those nightmares where my father is leading me into the forest? And, then, when I remembered seeing my mother lying on the floor with him standing over her. For god's sake, I remember smothering a baby named Carl. You made me remember that, Doctor. You!"

"Jessica, you can't be right. It doesn't make any sense. Jack Willerton was not your father. His wife wasn't your mother," Dr. Bentley stated emphatically.

"That's my point," Jessica cried out. "If Jack Willerton wasn't my father, then why am I remembering things that happened in his house?

What if that is his wife – who might be my mother, by the way - lying dead on the floor? What if he killed her?"

Dr. Jason Bentley reached over and picked a pipe up off the little end table next to his chair. He gently tapped the loose tobacco out of it into a glass ashtray.

Jessica silently watched him, realizing he was killing time while trying to answer her questions. Finally, he laid the pipe down and looked at her. He sighed deeply and smiled gently.

"I don't have a fucking clue," he said.

Jessica broke out laughing at his comment. He grinned and joined her. "Sorry," he said.

Jessica smiled. "Thanks for that," she said. "I was getting way too upset."

"Not at all, Jessica. You have every right to be concerned. It's all so very confusing. You seem to be having the memories of someone else – of another little girl."

"Perhaps, but I'm beginning to wonder if that's true. Maybe, I am that other little girl."

"You mean you think you might have multiple personalities? I don't think that's the case."

"No," Jessica replied. "I meant what if that little girl is actually me? What if I did have a baby brother named Carl? Since I started remembering, little bits and pieces of memories have flitted through my head. I'm not sure what is true and what isn't. It's all mixed up in there, but there are just too many coincidences to toss this idea aside as being total nonsense."

"I don't believe for one minute this is nonsense. I

think you do believe what you are telling me."

"Do you, Doctor? Because, there's more."

Dr. Bentley sat back in his chair and looked concerned. "There's more?"

"A lot more."

"Go on," he prompted.

"Peter and I dug up Carl's grave."

Dr. Bentley stared at Jessica. "You did what? I couldn't have heard that right."

"We dug up his grave. Guess what we found?"

"I couldn't begin to guess, Jessica. Just tell me."

"Nothing. We found absolutely nothing. What do you think of that?"

Dr. Bentley looked flabbergasted. "You didn't find a body?" he asked.

"Nope. No body. Nada. The coffin was empty."

"I see. So, what exactly do you think happened to it?"

"I'm not sure, but I think I'm putting the pieces together. After Peter and I left the Willerton farm, I started thinking about another grave marker I saw there for another Willerton child. All the letters weren't clear, but the ones I could read indicate that this could be Claire Ann Willerton's grave. And, Doctor, this child died the same day as Carl and was six years old when she died."

"Then, it certainly isn't you, as you are alive and well and sitting right here in front of me," Dr. Bentley stated, smiling.

"Or, that grave is empty, too, Jessica replied.

"You're probably wrong about that, Jessica."

"Well, that is exactly what I intend to find out."

Chapter Eighteen

Rachel Willerton stood and watched as Judge Finley entered the courtroom and took his seat behind a massive desk.

"You may be seated," he stated and looked down at the papers on his desk. He looked over at the prosecution's table. "Mr. Golden, I understand that you offered a plea agreement to the defendant. Is that correct?" he asked.

"It is, Your Honor," D.A. Mitch Golden replied. "Unfortunately, the defense has declined our offer."

Judge Finley frowned and looked over at Peter Fisher. "Is that correct, Mr. Fisher? You didn't accept the State's offer?"

Peter Fisher stood to address the judge. "We did not, Your Honor."

"Then, am I to understand that you plan on moving forward with your not-guilty plea?"

Peter looked at Jessica, who was sitting next to him at the defense table. She glanced up at him and slightly nodded her head. "No, Your Honor, we request that our original plea of not guilty be changed to not guilty by reason of temporary insanity," he replied.

"So, you're gonna try that old "She was only nuts for the few minutes it took to kill her old man" plea. Is that correct, Ms. Patterson?"

Jessica jumped to her feet. "Your Honor, I object to that terminology. It diminishes and mocks our client's wish to change her plea. We can, without a doubt, prove that Ms. Willerton was abused over a period of six years by her father. This continuous abuse brought her to a breaking point, causing her to snap under the pressure. She believes she could possibly have killed her father. I would further like to add that Ms. Willerton does not, however, have any recollection of this horrific event."

"If that's the case, Ms. Patterson, why is she changing the plea?"

"Truthfully, Your Honor, she would rather plead not guilty. She's confused and depressed about what happened to her father. Although she is positive she could not have done this, she does admit to having memory lapses on occasion. Therefore, given the evidence the prosecution has against her and the fact that they cannot find the parties who actually committed this crime, we have decided it would be in her best interests to change her plea."

Judge Finley looked at Rachel and noticed a small tear running down her cheek. "Ms. Willerton?"

Rachel stood. "Yes, Your Honor."

"What do you want?" Judge Finley asked her.

Rachel looked confused. "I don't understand what you mean, Judge," she said.

"It's very simple. Are you guilty or not guilty? Did you do it or not?"

Peter and Jessica were on their feet, both starting to address the judge.'

"Stop," Judge Finley yelled, obviously upset at being interrupted. "One at a time. Mr. Fisher, you wish to say something?"

"Yes, if I may, Your Honor."

"Go ahead."

"I'm sure you are aware that you can't ask her

that, Judge. So, I object to those questions."

Judge Finley smirked. "You do, do you? Well, too bad. However, I'll rephrase the question." He looked at Rachel and smiled. "My dear, do you wish to plead not guilty by reason of temporary insanity or not guilty? Your attorneys seem to think you went a little nuts and killed your father. Do you agree with them?"

Rachel looked over at Peter and Jessica, not sure what she should say. "I guess," she finally replied.

"You guess what? That you agree with them?"

Rachel looked down at a yellow legal pad and watched Peter write 'say yes'. She looked over at Judge Finley. "No, Sir," I don't."

Peter moaned softly. Jessica glanced up at Rachel and shook her head in disgust.

Judge Finley grinned. "Looks like you just upset your attorneys. So, tell me something, Rachel."

"What's that, Sir?"

"How would you like to plead? In your heart, knowing what only you can know, how would you like to proceed in this trial?"

"I'm not guilty. I'm sure I didn't do it. I sure don't think I'm temporarily insane. I mean, Judge, I didn't do it and I'd like to be found innocent."

"Request for a change of plea from not guilty to not guilty by reason of temporary insanity is denied."

Jessica stood and faced Judge Finley. "Do you have any idea of what you've just done, Judge?"

"You are totally out of line, Ms. Patterson. Your client made her choice. Now, deal with it."

"Your Honor, I am requesting that you recuse

yourself from this case.

Judge Finley turned and looked at the bailiff. "Call the next case, will you Mike."

"Your Honor!" Jessica exclaimed. "I'm not finished."

"You are more than finished here, Ms. Patterson."

"May I speak to you in private, Judge?" Jessica asked.

"Does it concern this case?" Judge Finley asked.

"Of course, it does, Your Honor," Jessica replied.

"Then, no." He turned to the bailiff. "Mike, please call the next case." He glanced over at Jessica, who was glaring at him. "Is there anything else, Jessica?" he asked.

Jessica started to say something, changed her mind, turned, and walked out of his courtroom.

Peter was pacing back and forth, waiting for Jessica to join him in the small conference room off of the courtroom. Rachel was listening to her iPod, and tapping her feet, keeping time to the music only she could hear.

Suddenly, the door pushed open and slammed into the wall behind it. Jessica stood in the doorway, staring at Rachel. Peter stopped pacing and looked at her. "It's bad, isn't it?" he asked her.

"Take those damn things out of your ears," Jessica demanded.

"She can't hear you," Peter said.

Jessica walked up to Rachel and roughly pulled an earbud out of her right ear.

"Ouch," Rachel yelled. "That hurt. What's wrong with you, anyway?"

"What's wrong with me, you little idiot? You wanna know what's wrong with me?" she yelled. "Well, I want to know what's wrong with you. Do you have any idea what you just did in that courtroom?"

"I'm not nuts. I told you that before. I don't want people thinking that I'm crazy."

"Jessica, calm down, will you?" Peter said. "And, shut the door."

"Really, Peter? You think I should calm down? Well, I think you should be more upset."

"It's not going to help anybody if I fly off the handle," Peter told her. "What's done is done. Now, we have to figure out a way to fix it."

Jessica sat down next to Rachel. "Why did you say that to the judge? We agreed that the best way to go was with the insanity plea."

"I know, but I didn't kill him, and I know I'm not crazy. I'm sorry, Jessica. I'm just so mixed up. Please don't be mad at me."

Jessica looked up at Peter and shrugged. "You're right. The damage is done. Now, we need to figure out how to fix it so Rachel doesn't spend the rest of her life in prison."

"All Rachel has to do is take the stand and have the same breakdown there that we saw a couple of days ago. If she can duplicate that, she'll have every one of those jurors eating out of her hand."

"So, everything's gonna be okay?" Rachel asked. "You're still going to be my attorneys?"

"Of course, we are," Peter told her. "Don't you

worry about a thing. Hopefully, in a few months, when this trial is over, you'll be a free woman."

"And, I'll be able to go back home to the farm?" Rachel asked him.

"Why would you want to?" Jessica inquired, surprised at Rachel's question.

"Because it's my home, that's why."

Chapter Nineteen

Jessica and her best friend, Suzanne, were sitting in a booth in the back room of Mitchell's Bar and Grill, in downtown Iron Mountain. It was the first time they had seen each other since Suzanne's wedding.

"Thanks for meeting me," Jessica said. "How was the honeymoon? It doesn't seem possible that you've been married almost two months already."

"I know," Suzanne agreed. "Time is going by so fast. And, to answer your question, the honeymoon was wonderful. Jessica, you've got to go there someday. Fiji is an absolute tropical paradise. We stayed in this thatched hut that was built on stilts, with the water just a few feet under us. It didn't look like much from the outside, but the inside was luxurious. We were treated like royalty from the time we got there until we left. You'd love it."

"I'm glad you had a good time. Maybe, someday I'll be able to take a vacation, but that's looking a long way off."

"How is your case coming along? Are you going to start jury selection soon?"

"No, you don't. We're not talking about me today. Today is all about you. I want to know everything you did after you left the reception. And, don't leave anything out," Jessica said, grinning.

An hour and fifteen minutes later, Suzanne looked at her watch and said, "I'm sorry, Jessica. I've got to get back to work. How about I stop over tonight?"

"No, I'm the one who is sorry. This wasn't supposed to turn into a 'Jessica has got a big problem' lunch. How did we get from you to me, anyway?"

"I'm glad we did," Suzanne said. "Your story is a lot more interesting than my honeymoon."

Jessica grinned. "I don't see how you can begin to compare the two. Your story has love and romance and sex and we all know that sex trumps - well, everything."

Suzanne grinned. "If that's the criteria, then I do win."

"Absolutely. And, you don't think I'm just a little crazy, after everything I just told you?" Jessica asked her.

"Oh, no. I've always thought you were a little off your rocker," Suzanne said, jokingly.

"Thanks a lot," Jessica replied, laughing.

"It's too bad that Doug is still holding a grudge. Will you ask him to recuse himself?" Suzanne asked Jessica.

"I have to. I can't see that anything will go in Rachel's favor with him trying the case. If he's on the bench, I'll be fighting two battles, and that's not fair to Rachel."

"Well," Suzanne stated, "it was a bad break up. He did expect to marry you, you know. By the way," she continued, changing the subject, "it seems that your doctor – Bentley, right? – has done a good job so far."

"I like him. I was hesitant at first to let him

hypnotize me, but it worked. I've remembered some things that happened when I was young. The problem, Suzanne, is that I'm just not sure they happened to me. How could they? I guess now it's just a matter of sorting out what's real and what I've dreamt or imagined."

"Are you still having nightmares?"

Jessica shook her head yes. "I am. Here's the thing, though. I'm not in a forest anymore. In these nightmares, I'm about six years old and . . ."

"Like you were in your other nightmares," Suzanne interrupted.

"Right. But, in these dreams, I'm in this big wooden box and I can't get out. I scream and scream, but no one comes and lets me out." Jessica met her gaze, then, lowered her eyes. "It's a coffin, Suzanne. I'm in a coffin and I'm buried alive."

The phone rang at four-thirty in the morning, waking Jessica. She reached for her cell and mumbled, "What?"

"It's Peter. Are you awake?"

"I am now. Do you know what time it is?" Jessica asked.

"It's four-thirty. I'm sorry I woke you, but this couldn't wait."

Jessica yawned and sat up, resting against her headboard. "It better be important, Peter."

"It is. Are you ready?"

"For crying out loud, spit it out. What is it?"

"They found Ted Williams."

Jessica jumped out of bed and started pacing

118

back and forth. "Are you kidding me? My god, that's great news. Where? Where did they find him?"

"It's not so great, Jessica."

"What do you mean, Peter, that it's not so great? This is exactly what we hoped for."

"Ted Williams is dead. His body was found in Willerton Woods. Some hunters ran across the body – or, what was left of it."

"How long has he been dead?"

"I don't know. The coroner will determine that. Although, I heard he'd been out there for quite some time."

"What about Jillian Wickstrom? Is there any word about her?"

"I'm afraid not. For all I know, she may be out there rotting away, too."

"It's more important than ever that we find her, Peter. Hopefully, she's still alive."

"I know. Again, I'm sorry I woke you, but I figured you'd want to know about this as soon as possible."

"I'm glad you did. But, how did you find out? Who called you?" Jessica asked.

"I couldn't sleep, so I went over to Smiley's for a cup of coffee."

"Smiley's Coffee House by the police station?"

"That's the one. I go there a lot when I can't sleep. Anyway, I was there when the late shift ended and some cops came in for coffee. They were talking about a body being found by some hunters, up there in Willerton Woods. I eavesdropped on their conversation."

"Do you know when they found it? How did they identify it so quickly?"

"There was a wallet in one of the pockets. His driver's license and some credit cards were in it. There is one thing, though. . ." Peter hesitated.

"What's that?" Jessica asked.

"From what I heard, there was a lot of dried blood on his clothes."

"I would think that the rain would have washed most of it away," Jessica commented.

"He was lying face down when they found him. Anyway, I'm hoping that some of it is Jack Willerton's blood."

"Which would prove that Williams was there when Willerton was killed," Jessica stated.

"Exactly. I'm thinking that Williams might have been murdered on the same day as Willerton," Peter declared.

"But that doesn't make sense. If Jillian and Ted killed Willerton, then, who killed Ted? It would take a lot of strength to kill someone and drag the body into the woods."

"Or, maybe all three of them killed Willerton."

"What three are you talking about?" Jessica asked.

"Think about it, Jessica. Maybe, Rachel was part of it after all. Perhaps, after they killed Willerton, the two girls forced Ted into the woods and killed him there."

"I must say, Peter, you have quite the imagination."

"It's really not that far-fetched," Peter said.

"Willerton raped both those girls. They wanted revenge and they needed some muscle. So, they get Ted to help them. What they didn't need was someone who might break under questioning, and spill his guts. The best solution to that problem was to get rid of Ted when they no longer had any use for him."

"And, just how do you figure they lured him into the woods?" Jessica asked.

"Hell, if I know. I'm sure he didn't go there willingly. I'm guessing they will find that Ted Williams was shot."

"You don't know that. You're just making stuff up."

"How about betting a dinner that I'm right."

Jessica thought about it for a couple of seconds. "You're on," she finally said.

Chapter Twenty

"You seem distracted tonight," Dr. Bentley remarked.

Jessica, who was lying on the couch in his office, looked over at him. "Sorry, I guess I am distracted. We start jury selection tomorrow for Rachel Willerton's trial. For me, that's always the hardest part of this process. It doesn't make any difference how prepared you are - if you don't select the right people to serve on the jury, you're dead in the water before you even begin."

"I would assume that all it takes is one bad apple to spoil your case."

"You assume correctly, Doctor. I lost a case once where a woman swore that my client pushed her into an alley, ripped her panties off, and fingered her. I had a witness who testified that my client was in another town, at a bachelor party, when the crime was committed. Even so, he was found guilty. I learned later that there was a woman on the jury who convinced her fellow jurors to vote guilty. She told them that she was positive that he was the same man who had robbed her a few months earlier, but she couldn't prove it. Most of the jurors thought he was innocent of the crime he was on trial for. But they convicted him anyway, to make him pay for what he had done to their fellow juror."

"Was she also sexually molested?"

"No, she wasn't. Except for the location being the same, the crimes were totally different."

"What did you do?" Bentley asked.

"As soon as we found out what this woman had done, we appealed it, of course. The verdict was thrown out. The D.A.'s office decided not to retry, the judge reviewed the findings, and my client's verdict was dismissed with prejudice. But you know what's funny about this?" Jessica asked.

"I couldn't even begin to guess," the doctor replied.

"Although he was innocent of molesting my client, he actually was the man who robbed the juror."

"No kidding. So, what happened to him?"

"He's in prison on an unrelated charge. He held up a liquor store three weeks after he was released."

Jessica looked at the expression on Dr. Bentley's face and added, "No. I did not represent him if that's what you are wondering."

"It was. However, let's get back to you. Are you up to talking tonight or would you rather wait until your jury selection is over?"

"I'm here, so let's talk. Besides, there's no way of knowing how long jury selection will take. It could be a day or it could take a week. I feel like talking now."

"Good," Dr. Bentley said. "How are you sleeping?"

"I have no trouble falling asleep. It seems I'm practically out before my head hits my pillow. It's staying asleep that's the problem. I've had two nightmares this week. They're basically the same. In fact, they are exactly the same. Are you ready?"

"Please." Dr. Bentley said, as he reached over and turned on the recorder.

Jessica lay back on the couch and closed her

eyes. "In this nightmare, I'm dying. I'm having trouble breathing and I'm suffocating. I scream and try to claw my way out of a small wooden box, which, obviously, is a coffin. It's uncomfortable, as there are no cushions and the wood is hard. There isn't even a little pillow on which to rest my head. It's just a wooden box and I've been buried alive and I'm dying. But, it's light inside the coffin and I can see everything clearly."

"Where is the light coming from?" Dr. Bentley asked. "Can you tell?"

"Fireflies. There are dozens and dozens of fireflies inside the coffin with me."

"Fireflies." Dr. Bentley remarked. "Interesting. You know, they say that fireflies symbolize hope."

"I didn't know that," Jessica replied.

"There are those who believe if you are in a period of uncertainty or self-doubt, and you see fireflies in a dream, it indicates that hope may be coming." He waited for Jessica to continue. Finally, after a long pause, he said, "Would you like to continue?"

"I love fireflies," Jessica said, softly. "I go out at night with a jar and I try to catch them. But I always let them go. Daddy won't let me bring them into the house, you know. He doesn't like bugs in the house. Mama doesn't care, though. I miss my mama. Daddy says she ran away, but I don't think so. I think Daddy hurt her real bad when he hit her."

Dr. Bentley stared at Jessica. He waited, but she was quiet. From where he was sitting, he couldn't get a good look at her face and he wondered if she had fallen asleep. He waited a few more seconds, then, very quietly asked her, "How old are you, Jessica?"

Jessica didn't respond. The only sound in the office was a clock ticking away the seconds.

"How old are you, Jessica?" he asked her, again.

Still, there was no response. He rose from his chair and walked over to where he could see her face. She looked like she was asleep. He stepped back, confused, and wondered if she was sleeping or was in some type of trance. She had sounded like a little girl when she spoke - like she sounded when he hypnotized her.

"Jessica," he said quietly. "How old are you?"

He could see her eyes flutter under her eyelids, and she smiled. "Why are you calling me Jessica? That's not my name. My name is Claire Ann and I'm almost six years old."

Dr. Bentley's heart started pounding in his chest. He took a step back from the couch and stared at her, not sure if he should wake her or continue to talk to her. The latter won out, and he pulled his chair closer to the couch and sat down. He watched her take shallow breaths as she slept, wondering what his next question should be.

"Jessica, where are you right now?"

He waited, hoping she would respond. Nothing. Suddenly, he realized his mistake. "Claire Ann, when is your birthday?"

"November 16th," Jessica replied.

"That's only a few months away. How old will you be?"

"I already told you. I'm gonna be six years old."

"What do you want for your birthday? A new

125

doll, maybe?"

"I don't want any dumb doll. Dolls are for sissies."

"Then, what would you like?"

"I want a BB Gun."

Dr. Bentley, totally shocked by her answer, sat back in his chair.

"Who are you?" Jessica asked. "Do you know my mommy and daddy?"

"Why would you want a BB gun, Claire Ann? Aren't guns for boys?"

"That's what Mama says, too. But I want one so I can learn to shoot good. Daddy says if I learn to shoot good, someday he'll take me hunting with him."

Dr. Bentley jumped, as the phone rang. He glanced up at the clock and realized that Jessica's hour had passed thirty minutes ago. It was probably his wife calling, wondering when he would be home.

"Are you going to get that?" Jessica asked, looking over at him.

Dr. Bentley smiled. "Ah, you're awake. How do you feel?"

Jessica looked confused. "Awake? Did I fall asleep?"

"To be honest, Jessica, I'm not sure what you did. You might have fallen asleep, but I think you went into some type of trance. You acted and talked the same as you did when you were hypnotized. The same voice – everything – just like a little girl. Do you remember any of it?"

Jessica shook her head. "No. The last thing I remember is starting to tell you about my nightmares.

About being buried alive in that horrible coffin." She sat up. "And, fireflies. I remember telling you about the fireflies in the coffin with me."

"Yes, you told me about them. That's where I lost you. All of a sudden, you were a little girl again. Only, it wasn't you, Jessica. You called yourself by a different name."

Jessica waited for him to continue. Finally, she asked, "Well, what name did I call myself?"

"Claire Ann. You told me your name was Claire Ann and you were going to be six years old on November 16th. There isn't a chance that your birthday is on the same day, is there?"

Jessica smiled. "No, my birthday isn't on November 16th. My birthday is June 2nd.

"Well, then, I guess you and Claire Ann are two different . . ." Dr. Bentley looked at the expression on Jessica's face and stopped talking.

"Oh, my god," Jessica exclaimed. "Oh, my dear god. It can't be."

"What is it," Dr. Bentley asked, as he watched Jessica turn pale. "What did you remember?"

"The cemetery. Do you remember me telling you about the marker for a little girl? You know, the one we thought might be for Claire Ann Willerton?"

"Of course."

"If I remember correctly, it says she died in June 1990."

"Did it say when she was born?" Dr. Bentley asked Jessica.

"November 1984. She would have been six the following November." Jessica had a puzzled look as she glanced over at the doctor. "What is happening to me?"

Dr. Bentley shook his head. "I have no idea, Jessica. Either you are Claire Ann, or you're experiencing some type of dissociative identity disorder. But you're not following the normal symptoms of DID."

"What do you mean?" Jessica asked.

"Normally, what we see are two or more personalities in one person, both existing at the same time. They may or may not know that there is more than one personality present. One or both personalities can experience blackouts and may not recall what their other personality has experienced."

"Isn't that what's happening with me?"

"No. You're recalling memories of a little five-year-old girl. You haven't had any instances of another personality being present. And, so far, none of the memories you are remembering are after 1990, which is when she died."

"But, how would I know this stuff about her? I just don't get it."

"Well, perhaps that little girl's spirit wants you to find out what happened to her. Whatever it is, we've got to find out exactly what is happening to you."

"Really, Doctor? Her spirit? I'm afraid I don't believe in that nonsense. However, I know what I have to do next. I have to go dig up another coffin and find out if there's a body buried in it."

"I don't think that's a very good idea. You got lucky when you dug up that baby's grave. This time, someone may see you."

"I'll risk it. But, if I don't find Claire Ann's bones

128

in that coffin, I'm going to dig up every damn coffin in that cemetery."

Chapter Twenty-one

Jessica walked into the hospital room, saw Rachel lying in a bed, and yelled, "What the hell were you thinking?"

Rachel opened her eyes, saw it was Jessica who was yelling at her, and looked away.

"I've already read her the riot act," Peter told Jessica. "There's no sense in yelling at her again. She doesn't understand what she did wrong."

"Unbelievable," Jessica said, totally infuriated at Rachel.

Rachel, upset at being yelled at, glared at Jessica. "Peter is right. I don't get it," she remarked. "We talked about this. I thought we all agreed that this is what I should do. Now, you come running in here, screaming at me and telling me I shouldn't have done it. I wish you two would make up your minds."

Jessica glanced over at Peter. "Did we agree to this, Peter? I don't remember telling Rachel to slit her wrists, do you?"

"Of course, he does," Rachel exclaimed. "You told me to quit being happy and act depressed, like I wanted to commit suicide or something. And, then I said . . ."

"Stop! I know what we said, and we never told you to slit your wrists or any other nonsense. This was your idea. Not ours. Now, with this crap you just pulled, you'll be under a suicide watch and you'll have to meet with doctors to prove you're not crazy. You're the one who told the judge you wanted to plead not guilty. You're the one who told him that you aren't nuts. But, trying to kill yourself proves you just might be a little crazy."

Rachel looked crestfallen as she listened to Jessica. "But I thought . . ."

"Right now, I don't care what you thought. This was stupid, no matter why you did it. You could have killed yourself," Jessica exclaimed.

"No, I wouldn't have. I knew what I was doing. There's no way these little cuts would have killed me."

"I talked to the doctor, Rachel. He said that if the guard hadn't found you when she did, you would have bled out."

"No way," Rachel replied. "I don't believe it."

"You nicked the artery in your left wrist. So, believe it."

Rachel glared at Jessica. "Whatever," she muttered and looked away.

"Damn right – whatever," Jessica yelled. "Now drop the attitude." She looked at Peter, who was observing the exchange between Jessica and Rachel, and said, "We've got a lot of work to do."

"No shit. We have to try to fix this," Peter replied.

"You have any ideas?"

"Do you know how long she'll be in here?" Peter asked.

"Around a week. It all depends on what the shrink decides. She'll be moved to the psych ward later today."

"I'm not crazy, you know," Rachel exclaimed. "Why does everyone insist that I'm a nut job?"

Jessica looked at Rachel and shook her head. "I'm not getting into this with you again." She glanced over at Peter. "What time is it?"

Peter looked at his watch and frowned. "It's a little after eight. We've got to get moving. Jury selection starts at nine and we can't be late."

Jessica looked over at Rachel. "Do you understand what is going to happen now?" she asked.

Rachel shook her head yes. "I'm going to be moved to the loony ward," she said and started to cry. "I'm sorry, Jessica. Really, I am. I thought this is what you and Peter wanted me to do."

"Well, you thought wrong."

"Are you going to visit me tomorrow?" Rachel asked.

"I doubt they'll allow us visiting rights while you're in the psych ward, but I'll check it out."

"Jessica?"

"What now. We've got to get going."

"I really am sorry," Rachel told her.

Judge Doug Finley entered his courtroom at exactly nine o'clock, said good morning, and instructed everyone to sit. He glanced over at the defense table and frowned. "Mr. Fisher, where is your client?"

Peter stood and faced the judge. "I regret to inform you that she is in the hospital, Your Honor."

"What's wrong with her?" Finley asked.

"She tried to commit suicide, Your Honor. She'll be under a suicide watch and doctor's care, in the psych ward, for approximately a week."

"I see. Well, I want her in my courtroom while her trial is going on. Will she be here after we complete jury selection?"

"I'm not sure, Your Honor. It depends on how long that takes."

"Ms. Patterson."

Jessica stood and looked at Judge Finely. "Yes, Your Honor?"

"What do you think?"

"I think if you hadn't talked Ms. Willerton into changing her plea, we wouldn't be here today discussing this."

Judge Finley sat back in his chair and stared at her. Jessica fixed her eyes on him – a deadpan expression on her face.

"That was not my question, Ms. Patterson, and you are out of order. Any more smart remarks and I'll hold you in contempt."

Jessica, still looking at him, smirked. "Fine."

"Do you think this is funny?" he asked her, his face turning red.

"No, Your Honor," she replied.

"You are fined $1,000.00 for contempt and you better see to it that we don't have a repeat of this type of behavior or you might just wind up behind bars. Is that clear?"

"It is, Your Honor. I'll appeal that fine, by the way."

"Appeal all you want." Judge Finley hesitated, took a deep breath, and asked, "When do you anticipate your client will be able to attend her trial?"

"As Mr. Fisher already informed you, the doctors have indicated that Ms. Willerton will be in the hospital for approximately a week."

"Very well. We will begin jury selection today. If

we finish before her week is up, we will delay starting the trial until she is available. Is that agreeable with you, Mr. Golden?"

D.A. Golden rose from his chair. "It is, Your Honor."

"Fine, then let's get started selecting this jury."

"There's one more thing, Your Honor," Jessica said.

"What?" he yelled.

"I would like to inform you that I have made a formal request that you recuse yourself from this case."

"I see," Judge Finley said. "Do you think you have a valid complaint to remove me?"

"I think you know that I do," Jessica replied, softly.

Judge Finley stared at her for a few seconds, then broke eye contact and looked down at the papers in front of him. "Perhaps, you do," he muttered. "Let's take a fifteen-minute recess. I'd like to see the attorneys in my chambers."

Chapter Twenty-two

"So, you and the judge used to date," Peter commented. "That explains a lot."

Jessica glanced over at him, smiled, and turned back to concentrate on her driving. "I should have told you from the beginning that we had a bad break up, but I was hoping that he wouldn't act like a prick. I should have known better. Once a prick always a prick."

Peter turned his head towards the back seat and said, "Remember, whatever you hear here, stays here. Got it?

"Got it, Bro'. My lips are sealed."

"I appreciate your coming with us today. Digging up graves is hard work. Peter is good with a shovel, but I'm worthless," Jessica told him.

"I doubt that you're ever worthless. Right, Pete?"

Peter smiled. "You're right about that."

As Steven Fisher, Peter's brother, stared at the back of Jessica's head, questions buzzed around in his head. He wondered if she was single or married. Was she involved with anyone? When he saw her reflection in the rear-view mirror, he was curious as to where those big brown eyes came from - her mother or her father. He smiled, amused that he was feeling such an attraction to a woman that he had met less than an hour ago.

"A penny for your thoughts?" Jessica asked him.

He smiled. "Hardly worth a penny."

"We don't have much farther to go," Peter said, oblivious to the flirting that was happening between

Jessica and his brother. "The turn-off to the Willerton farm is just up the road."

"How many times have you been out here, Pete?" Steven asked.

"This is my third time. Jessica's, too. Right, Jessica?"

"That's right. This is the third time we're visiting this hell hole."

"Why do you call it that?" Steven asked her.

"Because, Steven, I think God forsake this place a long time ago and let the devil take it over."

"Please, call me Steve. The only person who calls me Steven is my mother when she's pissed at me."

"Steve it is," she said. "We know of two murders that took place here," Jessica continued. "Jack Willerton, Rachel's father, and Ted Williams. We found a grave for a woman, named Sarah, who could be Jack's mother, but she was reported missing years ago by Jack's father. Peter thinks Jack's father killed her. Don't you, Peter?"

"It's just a theory," Peter replied.

"Carl Willerton's coffin was empty. So, where's that body? We think Marie Willerton, Jack's first wife, is buried in the cemetery, too. There's a head marker that could be hers. But she supposedly also ran off years ago when Jack was just a kid." Jessica told Steve.

"That's a lot of unknowns," Steve commented.

"It is. The only thing that we're sure of is that Jack Willerton and Ted Williams were killed here and that we found an empty coffin. The rest is just speculation."

"Turn up here," Peter told Jessica, pointing to a turn-off to their right.

"I know, Peter," Jessica said.

"Oh!" Peter yelled, making Jessica jump.

"What the hell? You scared the crap out of me," Jessica exclaimed.

"Sorry. I just remembered something. You owe me a dinner," Peter told her.

"I do? For what?"

"Our bet. Remember? I told you that they would find that Ted Williams had been shot. Well, guess what? They found shotgun pellets in and around his body."

"Fuck!" Jessica uttered. "Whoops! Sorry about that, Steve."

"I've heard the word before, Jessica. No need to apologize."

"It makes sense," Jessica said. "A young girl, holding a shotgun on him, would certainly have been able to force him into the woods. Especially, one who was familiar with guns and hunting, like Rachel."

"Rachel told us that she used to hunt with her dad," Peter commented.

"She did. I wonder if Jillian also knows how to shoot," Jessica remarked.

"I guess we'll find out if we ever find her. So, where you gonna take me for dinner?" Peter said, grinning.

"How does Wendy's sound?"

"Oh, no, Jessica. You aren't gonna get by that easy. I want an expensive dinner in a nice restaurant," Peter said, laughing.

"I'll think about it."

Jessica gradually slowed down the speed of the car and came to a stop. "We're here," she said.

"Can I come along?" Steve asked her.

"Of course. We didn't bring you out here to sit in the car," Jessica told him.

Steve laughed. "I didn't mean now, Jessica."

"Oh. What then?"

"Would it be okay if I go to dinner with you and Peter?"

Peter looked questioningly at Jessica and then at his brother. Suddenly, he realized what was going on between them. "What do you think, Jessica?" Peter asked her.

"It's fine with me," she said, smiling. "But I'm not paying for his meal."

"How about I not only pay for my own meal, but I buy the wine?"

"Sounds good to me," Jessica told him. "Now, let's get to work, shall we? Peter, would you get the shovels out of the trunk?"

"I wonder if I could ask a question," Steve said, as the three of them started walking up the hill to the little cemetery. "I'm curious about something."

"Of course," Jessica said.

"Just why are we digging up a grave? I mean, what does this have to do with the trial?"

Jessica stopped walking and looked at Peter. "You didn't tell him why we're doing this?"

Peter shook his head no. "He didn't ask."

"I see," Jessica replied. She looked at Steve and

said, "This isn't so much about the Willerton trial as it is about me. I need to find out if there's a body in the grave I want you guys to dig up."

"Can I ask why? What does a body buried in a family cemetery have to do with you? And, why wouldn't there be one? I don't get it."

"It's complicated," she told him.

"I can do complicated," Steve replied. 'In fact, I'm pretty good at it."

Jessica smiled. "I guess you have a right to know, seeing as how you're digging up a grave for me. First of all, you should know that I'm not crazy. You may think I am when you hear this, but I'm not. Right, Peter?"

Peter grinned. "Whatever you say, Jessica."

Jessica looked at Steve. "Forget him. He's no help whatsoever. The thing is, Steve, I've been having nightmares for years and I'm pretty sure this farm and these woods are where they take place. I'm remembering things that happened to a little girl years ago. Bad things. I've been seeing a psychiatrist and we're trying to figure out how I could be recalling events that happened to someone else."

Steve looked confused. "I'm not sure I understand what you're telling me. Are you saying that you might be that little girl?"

"I don't know. It seems like it, but I can't be, which is why this is all so confusing. While I was hypnotized, I talked about having a brother, Carl, who died in 1990. He was only six months old when he died. But I never had a brother. It was his grave that Peter and I dug up the last time we were here. There

139

was no body in the coffin, Steve. It was totally empty."

Steve looked at his brother, who was leaning on a shovel, listening to Jessica. "You didn't think you should tell me about this?"

Peter grinned sheepishly. "I figured you'd find out when we got here."

Steve didn't say anything for a few seconds, thinking. "And, I gather, there's another grave here of a little girl and you want to see if there's a body in that one. Am I right?"

Jessica looked him in the eyes and smiled. "You got it," she said.

"Then, what are we waiting for? Let's start digging and find dem bones."

Chapter Twenty-three

"Water, lemonade, or beer?"

Steve straightened up, dropped his shovel, and stretched. "I'll have water, please. You can save me a beer for later, though."

"I'll have some water, too," Peter said. He threw a couple more shovels full of dirt out of the hole, took off his right glove, and reached for the bottle of water Jessica was handing to him. "Thanks," he said and took a long swallow. "That's better. Man, I was really thirsty."

Jessica handed a bottle of water to Steve, who was wiping the sweat off his forehead. "Damn, this ground is hard."

"Are you sorry you came?" Jessica asked him.

"Not at all. It's not every day that a beautiful woman takes me for a drive to the country so I can dig up a body. We should be hitting that coffin pretty soon. We're down quite a way," Steve replied.

"We should have reached it by now," Peter said. "The other coffin we found wasn't buried this deep."

"What if there isn't a coffin here at all? You said you found the grave marker in the grass. That doesn't mean that the grave was right beneath it," Steve remarked.

"I know," Jessica said. "I considered that, but I figured she would be buried next to baby Carl's grave, seeing as how they died at the same time. Please, just go a little farther down."

Jessica sat on the grass, watching Peter and Steve dig. After another five minutes, just as she was about to tell them to stop, Peter exclaimed, "I hit something. I think we found it."

"Thank goodness. I was about to give up." Jessica said. "My god, I'm shaking," she uttered. "I'm really nervous."

"We can quit if this is too much for you," Peter told her.

Jessica laughed nervously. "Are you kidding? There's no stopping now. I've got to know if there's a body in there."

"Well, we should know the answer to that in a few more minutes. Just hang in there."

The two men continued shoveling, clearing the dirt off the top of the coffin. Finally, Steve looked up at Jessica and grinned. "This is it; the moment of reckoning. Pete, it's a little crowded. Would you mind giving me some space? And, would you hand me the crowbar?"

Peter crawled out of the hole and handed Steve the crowbar. Jessica watched as Steve started to pry open the top of the wooden coffin, nervously waiting for him to say something. He swore as a rotted piece of wood broke in two. Using his hands, he tore the smaller piece of wood away and looked inside the small opening.

"I see clothes in here. It looks like it may be a dress," he yelled up at Jessica.

"So, she's in there," Jessica stated.

"I'm not sure. Hold on."

Do you see any bones?" she asked him. "A skeleton – anything?"

"Not yet. It's too dark."

"Can I help?" Peter asked.

"Nothing you can do right now. Wait a sec. It's loose."

Steve pulled the rest of the piece of wood away and stared into the coffin.

"What's in it?" Jessica inquired. "Do you see a body?"

"Give me a minute. I want to remove the other piece of wood," he told her.

Using the crowbar, he pried the second board off the top of the wooden coffin. "Well, I'll be damned," he declared.

Jessica and Peter stood at the edge of the hole and looked down at the open coffin.

"I don't fucking believe it," Peter murmured. "Why go to all that trouble."

Jessica stared, not believing her eyes. On the bottom of the coffin there was a child's bonnet, a dress, and a pair of girl's black patent leather shoes, all carefully laid out on top of a quilt. She looked over at Peter, a confused look on her face. "It's like she disappeared. It's as if she was there and then she wasn't. What am I supposed to think now, Peter?"

"The view is nice," Steve said, as he watched Jessica pick up the litter from their lunch and put it into the basket. "It's so peaceful here. By the way, thanks for lunch. It was great."

Jessica smiled at him. "It was just sandwiches and chips, Steve. Not that hard to make."

"Well, maybe it's the company that made it taste great."

"Or, it might be that you worked up a huge appetite doing all that digging." She looked down at the farmhouse and felt a little chill go through her body. "I don't see how you can say it's peaceful here. I find this whole area extremely unnerving. It's like something sucked the life out of it."

Steve studied her as she talked. She's so beautiful, he thought. Suddenly he realized that all he wanted was to put his arms around her and tell her that everything was going to be okay.

She glanced over at him and smiled. "Are they worth a penny now?" she asked.

Steve laughed. "I doubt a penny is enough. I think I could get a whole nickel for them."

Peter, who had walked behind a tree to relieve himself, walked over to Jessica and Steve and smiled.

"What?" Steve asked. "I know that smile and it means trouble."

"Not at all. I was just wondering if you guys would like to take a walk in the woods."

Jessica's head jerked up and she glared at Peter. "Why in the world would you suggest that?" she practically yelled. "You know I'm. . ." She stopped talking, her face turning red. "I'm sorry, Peter. I didn't mean to yell. It's just that I'm not comfortable with that idea. As you well know, I have an unnatural fear of woods. It's something I need to work on."

"Then, all the more reason you should go," Peter said. "Right, Steve? We don't have to go far. I promise. This may help you see there's nothing to be afraid of. Besides, you'll have two strong, brave men to protect you."

"I don't think so," Jessica said, hesitantly.

"We could see where that Williams kid was killed," Peter said.

"What do you think, Steve?" Jessica asked.

Steve shrugged his shoulders. "It's up to you. I wouldn't mind taking a little walk. It's only one o'clock and we've got some time to kill before we have to leave."

It was clear that Jessica was agonizing over her answer and that she was trying to fight her fears. She looked at Steve and gave him a weak smile. "What the hell. Why not?"

"Are you sure, Jessica?" Steve asked. "I don't want you to do anything you aren't comfortable with."

"I need to try this. I've been having nightmares for years about being lost in the forest and being scared out of my wits. Besides, I'm not passing up the chance to see a crime scene, even if there's nothing much left to see."

"Do you enjoy looking at crime scenes?" Steve asked her.

"I do," Jessica told him. "I don't know why, but I've had a fascination with them as long as I can remember."

"Maybe, you should have been a crime scene investigator," Steve said, smiling.

"Maybe, I should have. By the way, what do you do for a living?" Jessica asked him.

Steve grinned. "I'm a crime scene investigator."

Jessica stopped walking and looked at him. "You're kidding me. He's kidding me, right Peter?"

"Nope. He's been doing that for years."

"How come I never ran across you in court?"

"I live in Marinette. Work there, too. Didn't Peter tell you anything about me?"

"She never asked," Peter interjected.

"You're a cop and you're out here digging up graves. You're breaking the law. What if we get caught? You could lose your job," Jessica said.

"And, you're an officer of the courts. The same goes for you," Steve replied. "However, we are on private property and . . . Well, I'm not sure what the law is regarding this."

"I'm pretty sure it's more than getting our asses chewed out," Jessica remarked.

They stopped at the edge of the clearing and looked at the trees in front of them. Peter glanced over at Jessica. "Ready?" he asked her.

"I'm as ready as I'll ever be," she said.

"Atta girl," Peter said. "Let's put on our jackets. No sense in giving the ticks a free meal."

Jessica took a deep breath and let it out. "Okay, guys, let's go exploring."

Chapter Twenty-four

"My god, these trees are huge," Steve commented.

"Some of them have probably been here for hundreds of years," Peter said. "There's a fortune to be made right here. I'm surprised none of the Willertons ever got into the logging business."

"Do you know where we're going?" Jessica asked. "It's easy to get lost in here. Did you bring a compass? We should have brought a compass with us. It's a lot cooler here than out in the open, isn't it?" She stopped walking. "Did you hear that? I think I heard something."

Peter and Steve looked at her. "Do you want to go back?" Steve asked. "It's obvious you're not comfortable being here."

Jessica closed her eyes and took a deep breath. "I'm sorry. I'm fine. I was just having a bad moment. I'll shut up."

Peter laughed. "That will be the day. I don't think it's possible for you to shut up. But, don't worry about it. If it helps you, then, by all means, chatter away."

Jessica smiled at him. "Thanks, Peter. By the way, how do you know where Ted Williams was killed?"

"I have a friend at the District Attorney's office. He talked to him and got the location. It's not that far."

"Do you think there'll be anything to see?"

"I doubt it," Steve said. "He was murdered months ago. I'm sure everything has been removed by now."

"I guess," Jessica replied.

"Would you like to hear an interesting fact?" Peter asked.

"I'd love to," Jessica told him.

"Jack Willerton's great grandfather, Seth Willerton, was about as dishonest as they get."

"Why would you say that?" Jessica asked.

"I found some old records in the basement at City Hall and came across copies of some Homestead Affidavits. I have to say that it made some very interesting reading."

"What did you find?" Steve inquired.

"At the time that old Seth applied to take advantage of the Homestead Act, it seems that an individual could be allotted up to 640 acres of land. That amount decreased over the years, by the way. Anyway, over a period of just a few months, by forging the names of his relatives, Seth managed to obtain over 10,000 acres of adjoining land."

"That's almost. . ." Steve thought for a second and grinned. "That old bastard got himself almost seventeen square miles of land."

"That's correct. I don't understand why he didn't get caught. It might be that Registers at the Land Offices moved around a lot. Whatever the reason, he managed it."

"This land?" Jessica asked. "Where we are right now?"

"You got it," Peter told her. "The requirements were that you had to be the head of your household or at least twenty-one years old. You had to live on the land, build a home, and farm the land for at least five years. After that, it was all yours. Oh, I almost forgot. Single women could also qualify."

"That would be a lot of work for one person," Steve said. "Is there more than one house on Willerton's property?"

"Not that I'm aware of. He cleared the land so he could farm, and he built that log cabin, which, remarkably, is still standing after all these years."

"The house where Rachel was abused. That place should be burned to the ground," Jessica added.

"I agree," Peter added. "I believe he started clearing another area, but when he realized that no one was checking to see if he was complying with the rules, he stopped and concentrated on just the one farm."

"That's just conjecture on your part," Steve stated.

"Not really," Peter commented. "I flew over this property not so long ago. There are a couple of open areas with no trees. It's very possible that Seth or one of his offspring started to clear out these areas, but never settled there."

"So, there are almost seventeen square miles of trees, just waiting to be cut and sold. It looks like Rachel is a very wealthy young woman," Jessica said.

"It kinda makes you wonder if she knows that, doesn't it?" Peter said.

"Money could be another motive for killing her father," Steve commented. "Sex and money. Tell, me, Jessica. Do you think she killed him? Or, helped?"

"I honestly am not sure. One minute I think she

could have done it and then the next, I don't believe she did. Usually, I have pretty good instincts about my clients, but Rachel is a puzzle."

"Well, I think she did it, but Jessica told me I can't say that. I have to keep my opinions to myself."

"That's exactly right," Jessica stated emphatically.

"We're here," Peter said, indicating the area where Ted Williams had been shot. "Look. There's a piece of crime scene tape still tied to that tree over there."

"Except for that, all I see are a lot of trees," Jessica commented.

"I didn't think we'd find anything," Steve said. "But, do you realize what you've just done?"

Jessica looked at the two men and grinned. "I just walked into a forest filled with huge spooky trees."

"And.. . ..?"

"And, what?"

"You didn't die or get attacked and nothing horrible happened to you, did it?" Peter replied.

"You're right," she answered. "But I have two strong, brave men with me"

"I'm going to go look around a little," Peter said. "Maybe, I'll find something the cops missed."

"I think I'll stay here," Jessica said. "What about you, Steve?"

"I'll stay here and keep you company."

"Don't be silly. Go explore with your brother. I'll be fine."

"You sure?"

"Totally. Now go."

"Okay. Pete, you go that way and I'll head in this direction. Let's meet back here in twenty," Steve said.

"You sure you're okay with this?" Peter asked Jessica again.

"I'm fine," she said, smiling. "Go. Have fun or do whatever it is boys do in the woods."

"I'm starting to get worried," Jessica said. "It's been almost an hour and a half since he left."

"I'm sure he's okay. Steve knows what he's doing. He was a boy scout and he's camped out in the woods since we were kids. He hunts, too. I wouldn't worry about him."

"Do you have your phone with you?" Jessica asked.

"No bars. I checked."

"So, you are worried," she stated.

"No, I checked to see if I had any messages."

"I think he's lost, Peter. Maybe, we should yell or something so he knows where we are."

Peter hesitated. "I suppose we could try it. He could have gotten turned around or something. It probably wouldn't hurt."

"Together, then," Jessica said, and they started yelling Steve's name.

"Quiet. Did you hear something?" she asked Peter.

Peter stood still and listened. "All I hear is the wind blowing through the trees," he said.

"I thought I heard someone yell," Jessica told him.

"You did," Steve said. Jessica and Peter turned

around and saw Steve walking towards them. "It was me."

"Thank God," Jessica said. "We were getting ready to call out the National Guard to come and find you."

"Do you have any bars on your phone, Pete?" he asked, ignoring Jessica's comment.

"No, I don't." Peter looked at the expression on Steve's face. "What's the matter? What happened?"

"We need to get the police out here," Steve said. "I found some bones, and they look like they could be human."

Chapter Twenty-Five

"There's nothing more we can do here. Let's go," Peter said. "Are you coming, Steve?"

"No. You guys go ahead. I'm gonna stick around here for a while. I'll catch a ride back to Iron Mountain with Mac."

"Are you sure we're not in trouble for being out here?" Jessica asked him.

"Just stick to the story. You're Rachel's attorneys. We drove out here to take another look at where Jack Willerton was murdered, took a walk in the woods, and found the remains of a body."

"What if they notice that a grave has been dug up?"

"I won't mention it if you don't. There's no reason for them to head over in that direction. The shovels are in your trunk, so they didn't see them. Even if someone sees the open grave, it doesn't mean that we did it."

Jessica shook her head. "I don't know. Cops aren't dumb. I'm sure they'd put two and two together and figure out it was us."

"Thanks for the compliment. Seriously, don't worry about it. I'll handle it if it comes up. Now, get out of here and go home. I'll talk to you later."

The only noise in the car was the humming of the tires on the highway. Jessica, deep in thought, flinched at the sound of Peter's voice. "Sorry. What did you say?" she asked.

"I asked if you were okay," Peter told her. "You're

unusually quiet."

"Just thinking, that's all. My mind is going a mile a minute."

"I would think so. Do you think they'll be able to identify the body?" Peter asked.

"I have no doubt that it's Carl Willerton. He was only six months old when he died and the skull Steve found was definitely from an infant. We know his coffin was empty. Who else could it be?"

"You could be right. DNA testing will prove it for certain. Do you think they'll try to match it to Jack Willerton's DNA?"

"Maybe. I'm going to request it if they don't." Jessica answered. "If nothing else, it would show if they are related."

"Jeez, Jessica. Who would do a thing like that? Who could dump a baby in the woods like trash? It kinda makes me sick to my stomach just to think about it."

"Do you think they'll find more bones?" she asked.

"Who knows? I'm sure the animals scattered most of them. I'm surprised that Steve found any of them, after such a long time. You would think that whoever did this could at least have buried that baby." Peter commented.

"None of it makes sense. There's an empty coffin with no baby in it and a dead baby rotting away in the woods. Why not bury the baby in the coffin? Where the hell is the body of the little girl? And, why take the time to bury coffins with no bodies?" Jessica exclaimed.

"I'm as confused as you are," Peter said.

"Well, I think the whole area should be searched. And, I mean every damned last mile. Who knows how many more bodies could be buried out there."

"They're going to find that out that we unearthed that coffin, you know," Peter said.

"I know. I wonder how Steve is going to handle that."

"I'm not too concerned about it, "Peter told her. "He's good, Jessica. They'll be thanking him before he's done telling his story. In fact, I bet you anything that he'll tell them about it before they find out about it on their own. You know, get ahead of it."

"What can he possibly tell them that will justify us coming out here and digging up coffins?"

"He'll find a way," Peter said. "Don't worry about it."

Jessica pulled over and parked in front of Peter's apartment building. "We're here."

"It seems that each time we make this trip, it gets shorter."

"And, it always seems to take longer to get where you're going than the drive back home," Jessica added.

"This has turned into a mess, hasn't it? We really haven't found anything that will help Rachel and prove that she didn't kill her dad."

"I know," Jessica replied. "Actually, I feel kind of guilty bothering you with my problems. It's just that I've had this breakthrough with Dr. Bentley about my nightmares and I need to find out what's going on. But, now, I'm more confused than ever."

"Don't feel guilty. It's like trying to solve an old

murder mystery. I can't tell you how interesting it's been researching old records and trying to find out more about the Willerton family. I love doing that kind of stuff. Plus, you never would have met Steve if I hadn't been helping you."

Jessica smiled. "You do have a very nice brother. I enjoyed meeting him."

"And, I'm pretty sure he enjoyed meeting you."

"When do you think he'll be back?"

"If I know Steve, he'll stay there until everyone leaves or calls it quits for the night. He's staying with me this weekend, so I'll find out what he knows when he gets here," Peter said.

"You'll call me, then?" Jessica asked.

"Not if it's late."

"I don't care how late it is when he gets back. Call me. Please."

Peter reached for the door handle, turned, looked at Jessica, and smiled. "I'll call you. Good night, Jessica."

Jessica smiled back at him. "Good night, Peter."

Chapter Twenty-six

Jessica glanced at the clock again. It was five minutes after three. Steve had been talking nonstop for the past three minutes.

"Tell me again," she prompted.

"I'm telling you that you don't have to worry about it," Steve said. "I explained to Mac Littlefield what was going on. I told him about your premonitions that the graves would be empty."

"And, you're sure you can trust him?" Jessica interrupted.

"He's an old friend. So, yes, I trust him."

"I know Mac Littlefield. Kind of, anyway. We've crossed paths throughout the years. He seems to be nice."

"He is."

"Why would he help? I don't understand how you got him to help you."

"Jessica, I know you're half asleep, but listen to what I'm saying. I took him aside and asked if I could talk to him when they finished up for the evening. I explained everything we did and why we did it. When the realization hit that he could have several unsolved missing person cases, plus some missing bodies, he agreed to help me. In a few days, I want you to ask permission to start digging up that cemetery."

"On what grounds? No judge is going to allow that."

"Mac Littlefield thinks they will. So, do I. We just have to be sure it's presented to the right judge," Steve said.

"This is crazy, Steve. This has nothing to do with Rachel's case. Digging up the Willerton family cemetery isn't going to help clear her."

"I think there are more empty graves," Steve told her. "Didn't you tell me that a couple of women that disappeared may be buried there? Or, at least there are markers for them. What if those coffins are empty, too?"

"What if they are? There's nothing anyone can do about it now," Jessica pointed out.

"Perhaps old Peter Willerton went after his runaway wife, Sarah, found her, and killed her."

"Jack's mother," Jessica stated.

"Right. And, then Jack's first wife, Marie, takes off, but we're pretty sure she's buried in that cemetery, too. Or, at least we're supposed to think she is."

"I saw Jack kill her in my nightmare."

Steve was quiet.

"Steve? You still there?" Jessica asked.

"Sorry. I was thinking. Do you have any idea where Rachel's mother is? What's her name?"

"Nancy something. And, no, we don't know where she is. We're trying to find her."

"Maybe she's out in those woods, too," Steve remarked.

"Who knows? Rachel has no idea where she is. She could be dead. Most mothers would eventually try to contact their kids, but Rachel has never heard from her." Jessica yawned. "You must be exhausted. I know I am," she said.

"I'll let you get back to sleep," Steve said.

"Thanks for calling me. I know you'd rather be in

bed."

"Not really. I enjoy talking to you."

"Me, too. Alright, then. I'll say goodnight. And, you're sure I don't have anything to be concerned about? I'm not going to have somebody knocking on my door with an arrest warrant?" Jessica asked.

"I'm sure. Like I already told you, Mac Littlefield and I stayed after everyone left and we filled in the grave. We're good."

"Thanks for everything," Jessica said.

"Good night, Jessica,"

"Good night, Steve," Jessica replied, pushed the end call button on her phone, curled up into a ball, and dozed off.

"Daddy, looked what I found," Claire Ann cried out, as she turned to see if her father was watching.

"Come over here," her father said.

Claire Ann walked over to where her father was kneeling down. "Why are you covering Carl up with all those leaves?"

Her father looked over at her and smiled. "What did you find? Was it something good?"

"I found a play house, Daddy. It's kind of little but I bet I could fit in it," she said.

Her father turned his head and looked over where Claire Ann had been standing. "Over there?" he asked.

"You wanna see?" she replied.

He picked up the bundle and walked over to where Claire Ann had been standing when she had called to him.

"You like it, Daddy?" she asked. "It's got a real shiny roof."

Her father bent down and tossed the bundle through the small opening into the small structure. "This is a deer blind, Claire Ann. This is where men hide when they go deer hunting and don't want the deer to see or smell them."

"Can I go in?"

"Of course, you can," he told her.

Claire Ann knelt down and started to crawl into the blind. Suddenly, her father put one hand under her chin and the other on the back of her head and twisted, breaking her neck and instantly killing her.

He stared down at his little girl. As he reached for her body, intending to throw it farther into the blind with Claire Ann's baby brother, she looked up at him.

"Why did you kill me?" she asked her father. "Is it because I hurt Carl?"

Her father, frightened, took a step backward and tripped, falling onto the hard ground. "How can you talk? You're dead."

A single tear rolled down her little cheek. "You can't kill me," Claire Ann said.

"I heard your neck snap. I saw you die."

"You will never kill me, Daddy. I'll never die."

As her father stood, his legs shaking, he reached into his pocket, pulled out a jackknife, and opened it. He grabbed Claire Ann and pulled her towards him. "Oh, yes, you will, you little bitch," he yelled and stuck the knife into her chest.

"No! Daddy, don't," she screamed, as she fell to the ground.

Her father took a deep breath and sank to the ground. His heart was pounding and sweat was running down his forehead. He sat there watching as Claire Ann took her final breath.

Finally, he stood and started walking slowly back towards his home.

"Someday, Daddy, I'll kill you. I'll kill you when you least expect it and. . ."

He slowly turned around, his heart beating out of his chest and his face ghostly white, and saw his little daughter standing there, smiling.

"Nooooo," he screamed.

"No!" Jessica yelled. Her eyes popped open and she sat up. Her heart was pounding. She took a couple of deep breaths, reached over, and turned on the light next to her bed.

"Son of a bitch," she whispered. "I need a cigarette."

Chapter Twenty-seven

"I think I'm Claire Ann Willerton and that Rachel Willerton is my half-sister," Jessica told Dr. Bentley, as she entered his office.

Dr. Bentley, who was sitting behind his desk, glanced up at her. "Good evening, Jessica. Looks like you're anxious to get started."

Jessica stood in the middle of the room and smiled. "Sorry. How are you tonight?"

"I'm well, thank you. What exactly do you mean when you say you think you're Claire Ann? What has happened, since I last saw you, that brought you to that conclusion?"

Jessica looked at the chair in front of Dr. Bentley's desk and, then, looked over at his couch. "Should I sit or lay down?"

"Whatever makes you comfortable."

Jessica sat down. "I'll start here. I may move to the couch, though."

Dr. Bentley smiled. "As I said, whatever makes you comfortable."

"I was out at the Willerton farm this weekend. We dug up Claire Ann."

Dr. Bentley reached for his pipe, waiting for her to continue. He started to tap the old tobacco into a large glass ashtray, then stopped, and looked into the end of the pipe.

"Did you hear what I said?" she asked.

"I did. I'm waiting for you to expound on that statement."

"She wasn't there. Oh, her clothes were there -

all pretty and laid out. Her bonnet was there, and her dress. Even her shoes and socks were there. But, was Claire Ann there? Of course, she wasn't. Because, I'm pretty damned sure that I'm Claire Ann," Jessica exclaimed, raising her voice.

"You found another empty grave? Interesting. That makes two now, doesn't it?"

"You find it interesting? That's what you have to say? Interesting? It's downright spooky. We opened up her coffin, Doctor. There was no body. Why would someone do that? Just bury some clothes. Why go to all that trouble?"

"Would you like a glass of water? You're extremely agitated, Jessica. You need to calm down."

Jessica stared at him and shook her head no. She stood up and started pacing back and forth. "I not agitated."

Dr. Bentley watched her for a few seconds, not saying anything.

Jessica stopped pacing. "I think I should lie down."

"I think that might be a good idea," Dr. Bentley said, agreeing with her. He watched as she made herself comfortable on the couch, then walked over and sat down in a chair next to her. "Should we start over?" he asked her.

"I guess." She closed her eyes, giving herself a moment to relax. "Okay. As I said, we dug up Claire Ann's grave and found it empty. Then, we took a walk in the woods and Steve found. . .."

"Wait. Stop. What do you mean when you say you took a walk in the woods?"

"I mean we took a walk in the woods. We decided to take a look at the area where Ted William's body was found."

"Who was with you?" Dr. Bentley asked.

"That's right. I left that part out. I was with Peter Fisher. You remember me talking about him, right?"

"I do."

"And, his brother, Steve. He's a cop from Marinette. He helped Peter dig up the coffin."

"A cop," Dr. Bentley stated factually. "A cop helped you dig up a grave. That's a little unusual and against the law, isn't it?"

"I guess," Jessica said abruptly and continued talking. "Anyway, we took this walk, and then Steve and Peter went to look around a little more and Steve found the remains of this little baby. And, I think it's Carl, but we won't know for sure until they do some DNA testing."

"Okay, stop for a second," Dr. Bentley said. "You found a corpse? A baby?"

Jessica took a deep breath. "Sorry, I'm all over the place. Yes, Steve found the remains of what appears to be a baby."

"So, you're assuming it's Carl. You don't know that for sure."

"I think it's obvious. His coffin was empty, just like Claire Ann's. Who else could it be?"

"You may be right. However, it might be best that you don't jump to that conclusion until you get some proof," Dr. Bentley said. "Now, let's address the walk in the woods and your hylophobia. How did you manage to overcome it?

164

"I think having Steve and Peter there helped. When I told them about my fear of woods, they said we should try it and that we would turn back if I got uncomfortable. They kept me between them like they were protecting me. At first, I was kind of scared, but Peter just kept talking and it distracted me. When we found the area where Williams was murdered, there wasn't much to see. After that, Steve found the remains of that baby. We called the authorities, told them what we had discovered, and they came right out. I wasn't even afraid when Steve and Peter walked me back to the farm. I'm not sure if I could have gone back there by myself, though."

"Where did he find the body? Was it close by?"

"I wasn't with Steve when he found it. Peter and I were starting to worry about him, he was gone so long. But it wasn't a body he found– it was just a skull and one or two bones. But there were definitely from an infant," Jessica told him.

"And, you think it's Carl, Claire Ann's little brother," Dr. Bentley stated.

"I do. I also think that my father tried to kill me. I think he took me into those woods and left me there to die."

"And, yet here you are, Jessica. Alive and well."

Jessica sighed. "I know. I know my father didn't try to kill me. He was a wonderful man. The truth is, Doctor, I really don't know what's going on. It's like this little girl, Claire Ann, is inside my head. I'm having her nightmares and remembering stuff about her when she was a little girl. I had a different nightmare Saturday night and, in this one, I see my father throw Carl's body – who I killed, by the way – into a deer blind that's in the woods. Then, he tries to kill me. Twice. But I don't die. He can't kill me."

"You mean he can't kill Claire Ann. It's not you, Jessica."

"I know. But, in my nightmares, it is me. Claire Ann and I are the same. I am Claire Ann."

"How does this nightmare end?" Dr. Bentley asked.

"She threatens him. She says she's going to kill him, and he runs away from her."

"Hmm. Interesting. Claire Ann is taking control. She isn't allowing him to hurt her. The roles are reversing. She's becoming the aggressor."

"You're right. At the end of my dream, he was terrified of her."

"What happened then?" Dr. Bentley asked her.

"That's it. I woke up. My yelling woke me."

"Is it vivid? This dream of yours?"

"Totally," Jessica replied. "And, I know I've been there before. I've been in those woods, at that exact spot, and I've been inside that deer blind."

"That's not possible," Dr. Bentley said.

"Then, how do you explain it, Doctor?"

Chapter Twenty-eight

Rachel Willerton had been listening to the prosecution's witness, Alfred Finnegan, the County Coroner, for over an hour and was having trouble staying awake. She glanced over at the jury and held back a grin. Old Whitehair, the nickname Rachel had given to juror number six, was sleeping. She poked Jessica in the ribs to get her attention and whispered, "Number six is asleep."

"Shhh," Jessica instructed her.

Rachel tried to concentrate on what Finnegan was saying, but his monotone voice was doing nothing more than to make her tired. She yawned and looked up at the judge. He's kinda sexy looking, she thought. She smiled at him, but he didn't notice as his attention was directed on her attorney, Peter Fisher, who had just made an objection.

Jessica looked over at her and realized that Rachel was actually trying to flirt with the judge.

"Stop that," Jessica whispered to Rachel. "The jury is watching you."

"I'm bored," Rachel whispered back. "Look at the jury. They're all about to fall asleep. Can't you interrupt or do something and make that man shut up?"

Jessica held back a grin. "We still have to cross. He'll be up there for a while. Pinch yourself if you think you're gonna fall asleep."

"I'm so bored," Rachel said. "Can't we take a break?"

"Quiet," Jessica told her.

The door that led to the judge's chambers opened, a man entered, and walked over to the judge's bench. He leaned over and whispered something in the judge's ear. The judge looked surprised, glanced over at Jessica, and turned to address the courtroom. "Mr. Golden," he said to the District Attorney, "I'm sorry to interrupt you during your examination of Dr. Finnegan. I've just received some news which requires my attention. Court will be adjourned until nine o'clock tomorrow morning." He hit his desk with his gavel and said, "Court dismissed."

Everyone in the courtroom was silent as they watched the judge leave the room. Rachel turned to Jessica and asked, "What just happened? Are we done for today?"

"We are. I don't know what information the judge received, but it may not have anything to do with your case."

"Let's go talk, shall we?" Peter asked. "We've got some things to go over."

As Peter and Jessica were gathering up their files, the bailiff walked over to their table. "The judge wants to see you in his chambers," he told them.

"What about?" Peter asked.

"I don't have that information. He told me to catch you before you left and tell you that he wants to see you." He glanced over at the D. A. "You, too, Mr. Golden. He wants to see you, too."

Mitch Golden stood, grabbed his briefcase, and started walking toward the judge's chambers. "I wonder what the hell is going on now?" he mumbled to himself, as he passed the defense table.

"We want to talk to Rachel before we leave. Can you put her in one of the conference rooms so she can wait for us there?" Peter asked the bailiff.

"No problem. Now, go see the judge. You know he doesn't like to be kept waiting."

Judge Oscar Talaki, who was sitting at his massive antique oak desk, didn't look up when he heard the knock on his door. "Enter," he yelled and continued reading.

"Is there a problem?" Peter asked as he entered the room.

Judge Talaki finished what he was reading, then looked up at the three attorneys, and removed his glasses. "You might say that, Mr. Fisher. I've just received some disturbing news and I'm not sure if it affects your case or not. I'm leaning towards not, but I need a little more information before I decide one way or the other."

"What would that be?" Jessica asked.

The judge motioned towards the chairs in front of his desk and said, "Sit."

He watched as the three attorneys got comfortable, then sat back in his chair, and picked up the piece of paper he had been reading. "Do you know what this is, Ms. Patterson?" he asked.

Jessica shook her head no. "I have no idea," she responded.

"So, you haven't been informed of the DNA results for that infant you found out there in Willerton Woods?"

"No, Sir, I haven't."

"I see," he said. He picked up the paper he had been reading and held it up so Jessica could see it. "This is a copy of the report. It seems that Jack Willerton was the baby's father. And, that makes Rachel Willerton, who is on trial in my courtroom, that little baby's sister. Well, I guess that would make her a half-sister, seeing as how that little baby and she had different mamas, but they're still sisters."

"Of course," Jessica said, agreeing with him.

"I know that you helped find that little baby, Ms. Patterson. What I don't understand is what you were doing out at that Willerton farm and in those woods. Would you care to explain that to me?"

"There's no question about Jack Willerton being the father?" she asked, ignoring the Judges question.

"No question. They managed to obtain enough DNA from the bone marrow to match it to Jack Willerton."

"That doesn't surprise me. However, it was Detective Steven Fisher who found the remains. I wasn't with him when he found them."

"But you were in the woods with him, right?"

"Yes, that's correct, Your Honor. We were at the Willerton farm and decided to take a look at the area where Ted Williams had been murdered."

"I see. Is there anything else I should know?" Judge Talaki asked.

Jessica hesitated before answering him. "I believe those remains belong to Carl Willerton," Jessica said. "He was six months old when he died in 1990."

Judge Talaki stared at her. "And, you know this

how?"

Jessica looked over at Peter, then back at the Judge. "I just know it."

"Mr. Fisher, do you know how Ms. Patterson knows this?"

"Kind of. I mean, she has a theory, but it's kind of complicated," Peter said.

"Well, I need to know and you're not leaving here until I know why you think you know who that infant is. Especially when nobody else had a clue before the test results."

Jessica sighed. "It's a long story, Your Honor."

"Well, then, I guess it's storytelling time," Judge Talaki told her.

"I'd like the District Attorney to leave first. Peter knows the story, so maybe you could excuse him, also," Jessica said,

"Your Honor, I will not leave," Golden said. "I have every right to know what's going on."

"I can guarantee that what I'm about to tell you has absolutely nothing to do with this case, Your Honor," Jessica said. "It's just very private."

Judge Talaki studied Jessica's face, trying to decide if she was telling the truth. "Mr. Golden, you are excused. I'll see you in court tomorrow morning. Mr. Fisher, you stay."

"But, Judge . . ."

"No buts, Mr. Golden," the Judge interrupted. "Goodbye."

D.A. Golden picked up his briefcase and as he walked by Jessica, he whispered, "I'll find out, anyway, you know."

Jessica glanced up at him and smiled. "Not if I can help it," she said.

Judge Talaki waited until Golden shut the door. "Go ahead," he told Jessica.

"Can this be off the record?" Jessica asked him.

"It can," he replied. "But before you start. . ." The Judge opened up the left bottom drawer of his desk and pulled out a bottle of bourbon. "You thirsty?" he asked Jessica and Peter.

An hour and ten minutes later, Judge Talaki was pouring himself his third drink of bourbon. "That's quite a story," he said and took a sip of his drink. "You sure I can't fix you another one?" he asked.

"I'm fine, thanks," Jessica answered.

"I'm good," said Peter.

"You haven't said anything," Jessica commented. "Is this going to affect our case?"

Judge Talaki sat back in his chair and gazed at Jessica. "That is indeed quite a story," he repeated. "You know that digging up those graves could have serious consequences, don't you?"

"We thought about that, Your Honor, but we did get permission from the owner of the property," Peter said.

Talaki grinned. "That's a fine line you're walking, my boy. Besides, Rachel Willerton is a minor."

"So, has this affected the trial?" Jessica asked again.

"I'm going to have to think on that for a while. Right now, Jessica. . . May I call you Jessica?'

"Of course," Jessica replied.

"Good. Right now, Jessica, this is what I'm going to do." He stopped talking and stared at a picture on his credenza.

"Your Honor?" Peter said.

"Sorry. You see that picture there?" he asked, pointing to the picture he was looking at. "That's my sister, Margaret. We called her Maggie. Sometimes, Magpie. I loved that girl. Anyway," he continued, "she was what you call psychic or second-sighted. People used to laugh at her, but nine times out of ten she was right in her predictions. She never married or had any children of her own. Damned shame, too. She would have made a wonderful mother." He took another sip of his drink.

"So, Jessica," he continued, "when you tell me that you're experiencing this little girl's memories, I believe you."

"I have to say I'm surprised, Your Honor. Most people would think I'm a little off my rocker. In fact, I've considered that fact myself."

"I would never admit this to the media, and what I'm about to say doesn't go any farther than this room. Understand? But I do believe that there is something out there that we don't understand. I think this Claire Ann person wants her spirit put to rest and she can't do that until the mystery of her death is solved."

"But, none of this is helping Rachel. It's just that we went out to that farm hoping to find something that would help our case, and all I've done is make things worse."

"Not really," Judge Talaki told her. "There may be more bodies missing from that cemetery. After all, you still don't know where Claire Ann's body is. Perhaps, those woods should be searched from one end to the other. Maybe, her bones are out there, too."

Jessica's heart started to race, wondering if she should ask the question. She looked straight into the Judge's eyes and said, "Could you do that?"

"What? Search the woods? That would be a big job for just one person, don't you think?" he joked and took another sip of his drink.

"What about a few cadaver dogs? If there are more bodies buried there, they could find them," Jessica suggested.

Judge Talaki grinned at her. "You want me to sign an order to search those woods, don't you?"

"Maybe. I'm just saying . . ."

"Stop talking. Let me think about it. I must be crazy to even consider this. I'd have to pass it by some people. The next thing you'll be doing is asking me to dig up that cemetery."

Jessica smiled. "Could you?"

Judge Talaki laughed. "You've got balls; I've got to say that."

"Can't blame a girl for trying, Judge."

"Well, one step at a time. I'll let you know what I decide, but as far as this trial goes . . .. Well, I don't think this will have any effect on it. I'll see you both in the morning.

As Jessica and Peter rose and started walking towards the door to leave, Judge Talaki said, "By the way, tell your client to stop trying to flirt with me or

I'm going to hold her in contempt. Got it?"

"Got it!" Jessica and Peter said in unison, as they left the room trying not to laugh out loud.

Chapter Twenty-nine

"Your Honor, at this time, I would like to make a motion that all charges against my client, Rachel Willerton, be dropped. The prosecution has finished the examination of his witnesses and, as I'm sure you will agree, has failed to meet its burden of persuasion."

Judge Talaki watched District Attorney Golden jump up from behind his table. "Your Honor, I object."

"Sit down, Mr. Golden. Mr. Fisher is still speaking and I want to hear what he has to say."

Golden gave Peter a dirty look and remained standing.

"I said sit down," Talaki told him again.

Golden hesitated, as if he was about to reply to the Judge, thought better of it, and sat down.

"Good choice," Talaki told him. "Mr. Fisher, would you care to continue?"

"Thank you, Your Honor. I believe that after reviewing the evidence that has been presented – or lack of, I should say – the prosecution has not met its burden of proof. Therefore, we ask this court to dismiss all charges against Rachel Willerton, with prejudice."

Judge Talaki sat back in his chair, thinking about the motion that Fisher had put before him.

"I tend to agree with you, Mr. Fisher. I, also, question whether Mr. Golden brought this case to trial too soon."

Golden, obviously angry, was on his feet once again. "I object, Your Honor. Mr. Fisher doesn't know what he's talking about. I believe that we have more than proved our case."

"Overruled. Although, I don't know exactly who or what you're objecting to.

"Mr. Fisher," Mr. Golden replied.

"Then, the ruling stands. There's no jury present in the courtroom, and, try to remember, Mr. Golden, that this is a juvie court. I don't even know why you're trying it. One of your assistants would have been more than capable to examine the few witnesses you have presented in this case.

"This is a first-degree murder case, Your Honor. I felt like it deserved to be treated like one."

"And, I'm beginning to wonder if I should even have allowed it to come to trial," Judge Talaki replied.

"Your Honor. . .."

"Mr. Golden, I'm going to stop you right there. It's already three o'clock. I'm going to adjoin for today and give Mr. Fisher's motion some consideration. I'll give you my ruling tomorrow. Court's dismissed."

"What do you think?" Jessica asked Peter.

"I think this is one fine Ruben sandwich," he replied.

"I agree," Jessica said. "But I was talking about Judge Talaki. How do you think he'll rule?"

"My best guess is he'll dismiss without prejudice. The D. A. didn't present an iron-clad case. There's a lot of wiggle room, as far as I'm concerned."

"I agree. He'll leave an opening for the D. A. to retry by dismissing without prejudice."

"Probably. But Golden is going to have to come up with a lot more than he has now," Peter stated.

"What's gonna happen to Rachel if the case is dismissed? She's only sixteen. She sure can't go back to the farm. Have you had any luck finding her mother?"

"I haven't really spent any more time on it. Although, Jessica," Peter said, "I wouldn't object to putting a private investigator on it. What do you think?"

"It couldn't hurt, but who's gonna pay for it? If you recall, we're doing this pro bono."

"We could front it, I guess. If Rachel is found innocent or the case is dismissed, she'll be worth a fortune," Peter pointed out.

"Only on paper," Jessica said. "Those trees aren't making any money just standing there."

"What about Jack Willerton's accounts? Those are frozen right now, awaiting the outcome of the trial. But I understand there's around sixty thousand in savings. Plus, there's the farm. She'll inherit that, too."

Jessica thought about what Peter had said. "Let's do it," she finally said. "Let's hire someone and see if we can find that mother of hers. Although, we should probably ask Rachel if that's what she wants. The woman did run out and left her to be molested by her father. There's a good possibility that Rachel doesn't want to have anything to do with her."

As Peter was about to take a bite of his sandwich, he suddenly looked over at Jessica, a questioning look on his face.

"What?" Jessica asked.

"What if you are Claire Ann? Do you realize what that would mean, Jessica?"

"I'm pretty sure I'm not her," Jessica replied.

"But what if you are? You'd own half of the farm and Willerton Woods. You'd be Rachel's half-sister."

Jessica laughed. "Little chance of that," she said.

"Why don't you get a DNA test and find out for sure?" Peter asked.

"That's a little out there, don't you think?" Jessica said, grinning.

"Do it!" Peter exclaimed. "That would explain so much about your nightmares and memories. You should do it."

Jessica stared at him. "That's crazy," she finally said.

"Is it really? Don't you want to know?"

Jessica sat back in her chair and shook her head. "I do. I mean, I don't think I am Claire Ann, but it would be a big step in finding out what's going on with me." She thought for a few more seconds and smiled. "You know what? I'm doing it."

"Yes!" Peter yelled, then, looked around the restaurant to see if anyone was staring at him. "Yes," he said again, quietly. "Good for you."

"But..."

"But, what? Are you having second thoughts already?"

"No. It's not that. But what if I find out that I am Claire Ann? I'd be taken off Rachel's case. It could be grounds for a mistrial."

"You may be right. Maybe, you should wait until after the trial is over before you pursue it," Peter said.

Jessica nodded, agreeing with him. "I guess that might be best. Are you done eating? I've got to get back to the office."

"Go ahead," Peter told her. "I'm about to have a piece of that delicious-looking pecan pie that I saw when we walked in."

Jessica grinned. "It did look good. Enjoy."

Peter watched as Jessica picked up her purse and walked out of the restaurant. I can see what Steve sees in her, he thought. She really does have a nice ass.

He caught the server's eye and motioned for her to come over to his table.

Chapter Thirty

It had been four weeks since Jessica and Peter had talked to Judge Talaki in his chambers about Jessica's premonitions. The Willerton trial was over – at least for now - and Rachel had been placed in a temporary foster home. She had petitioned the courts to be emancipated and would know the answer in a few weeks. The fact that she would be financially stable would probably sway the courts in her direction.

The Judge's ruling to dismiss without prejudice had been a gift as far as Jessica was concerned. Of course, there was always the possibility that the D. A. would find more evidence and decide to go forward with the case.

The detective, that Peter had hired to find Rachel's mother, had called Peter and told him that he had some leads on a couple of women who might be Rachel's mother. He was following up and would report back to Peter as soon as he had more information.

"It's a waste of money, you know," Jessica said.

"Probably. But, if we find her, Rachel would have someone to take care of her," Peter replied.

"Rachel doesn't need some stranger to take care of her. She needs someone to help get her head on straight. If the courts rule in her favor, they won't be doing her any favors. She needs help, Peter, and guidance from people who know how to deal with children who have been abused. What she doesn't need is to be allowed to run wild with a bunch of money to blow. My god, she's already talking about buying some fancy sports car. What in hell does anybody need a car like that for?"

Peter grinned.

"What's funny?" Jessica asked him.

"You mean like the one you have?" he said, teasingly.

Jessica started to say something, thought better of it, and stayed quiet.

Peter looked at the farmhouse. "She wants to come back here, you know," he commented. "She actually wants to come back and live here all alone in that hell hole of a house."

"I know," Jessica said. "If I had my way, I'd torch it. Burn it to the ground. I can't even imagine all the evil that went on in there."

"You want something to drink?" Peter asked as he reached towards the cooler.

"I'll have another beer if there's any left," Jessica said.

Peter took a beer out of the cooler, popped the top off, and handed it to her.

"Thanks," she said.

He opened one for himself and took a long swallow. "Do you think they'll find anything out there?" he asked, nodding his head in the direction of the woods.

"I don't know. It's a large area to cover and it's been years. I kinda doubt it," Jessica answered.

Peter and Jessica were sitting in fold-up lawn chairs, watching the activity taking place on the Willerton farm. They had been allowed to be there with the stipulation that they would stay out of any area that was to be searched. In other words, they could watch – not touch.

Early that morning a group of law enforcement officers had arrived with two cadaver dogs and had headed into Willerton Woods. They had two days to find the remains of Claire Ann Willerton. After that, the search would be called off.

Jessica looked over at the little cemetery. The graves, which had been unearthed the previous week, remained open, with piles of dirt alongside them. The two coffins that had been removed were still lying on the ground, opened and empty.

"It's sad, isn't it?" Peter asked as he saw the sorrowful look on Jessica's face.

"I can't help but wonder if all of this is my fault," Jessica said. "I should have left well enough alone. It was those damned nightmares."

"All you did was tell Judge Talaki your story. He managed all of this," Peter said, as he motioned towards the woods and the cemetery. "If anything, this should help you."

Jessica stared at the label on her beer bottle and, then, took a small sip. "Did you ever wonder who invented beer," she asked Peter.

Peter grinned. "Where did that come from?"

"I don't know. Just blew through my brain, I guess. It has, you know," she said.

Peter looked confused for a second, then, realized what she was referring to. "How so?"

"I haven't had a nightmare for a couple of weeks. I'm dreaming, but they aren't scary dreams. Oh, she's still with me. Claire Ann, I mean. Sometimes, she's playing with her dolls or her dogs. In one of them, she is helping her mother bake cookies. Sometimes, her baby brother is there, too. She's happier now. She tells me she's going to leave soon," Jessica said, her voice cracking.

Peter looked over at Jessica and was surprised to see tears running down her cheeks. "But, that's a good thing, isn't it?" he asked.

"I guess, Jessica replied. "Maybe, when all this is over, we'll both get some peace."

"You mean you and Claire Ann?"

"Uh-huh. She needs her spirit to be put to rest and I need a good night's sleep," Jessica said, smiling. She wiped the tears off her cheeks with the back of her hand. "Sounds stupid, I know, but, until she leaves this world, I'm pretty sure I'm stuck with her."

Jessica and Peter, hearing loud voices, looked over at the tent that had been set up by the search team.

"What's going on?" Jessica asked.

"I'm not sure, but they seem excited about something."

"Go find out," Jessica told him.

"They told us to stay clear, remember?"

"I'll go," Jessica said and stood up.

"Wait, Jessica," Peter said, stood, and took her arm. "I'll go with you."

Mac Littlefield looked up as he saw Jessica and Peter approaching the tent. "Shit," he muttered to himself.

He walked to the opening of the tent and waited. Jessica gave a little wave and stopped a few feet in front of him.

"Something I can do for you guys?" Littlefield asked.

"We heard the excitement and were wondering if you found something."

Littlefield frowned. "You're not supposed to be here, you know."

"Sorry," Jessica said. "We'll go back and wait."

Jessica and Peter started walking back to their chairs.

"Just a minute," Littlefield said.

Jessica and Peter turned around, looked at him, and waited for him to speak.

"We found some bones," Littlefield said. "They're bringing them in now. They could be animal bones, so we won't know for sure until an expert takes a look at them."

"Thanks. You'll let us know?" she asked.

"I will. I heard from your brother," he told Peter.

"Is he coming out?" Peter asked.

"Not today, but he said he'll be here tomorrow to help with the search. He asked me to tell you that he'll call you later."

"Thanks," Peter told him. He looked at Jessica and said, "There's nothing to do here. We might as well leave."

"But, it's still early," she said.

"And, it's getting cold and I'm tired. I'd like to call it quits for today," Peter said.

Jessica pursed her lips, thinking. "Okay, let's go. But you're driving. I'm tired, too."

Peter was surprised at what he had just heard.

"You're gonna let me drive that car of yours? You must be tired."

Chapter Thirty-one

Peter parked Jessica's car in front of his apartment complex and opened the car door. "See you tomorrow. We can take my car if you want"

"Steve is driving tomorrow."

"You talked to him?"

"I did," Jessica replied. "He said he'd like to be on the road by seven. I guess he plans on picking you up first. See you tomorrow."

As soon as Peter left the car, Jessica scooted over into the driver's seat and drove away. She reached over for her purse that was on the passenger seat, took out her phone, hit a number on speed dial, and waited until Dr. Bentley answered his phone.

"Jessica?"

"How'd you know it was me?"

"Caller ID."

"Do you have a minute?"

"I guess. What can I do for you at 5:30 on a Saturday afternoon?"

"Are you at your office?" she asked him.

"I am. I'm about ready to leave, though. We're having a thing tonight and I've put off going home about as long as I can."

"Sounds like you're looking forward to your evening," Jessica said, amused at his remark.

"I always look forward to seeing my wife - the dinner guests not so much."

"Relatives?" Jessica inquired.

"A brother-in-law and his family are coming over for dinner. He's okay, but his wife needs to see someone and get some help."

Jessica laughed. "What about you?"

"God, no. I'd wind up in jail if I had to spend an hour alone with her. But, enough of my trials and tribulations. What can I do for you?"

"I think Claire Ann is about to leave me and it's making me extremely sad."

"Why would you be sad?"

"Because I don't have the answers I need. I don't want her to leave until I know for certain that I'm who I think I am and not her."

"Do you want my advice? Or, do you just need to talk?"

"I'm not sure," Jessica answered. Then, after a slight pause, she said, "Your advice. I need to know if you think I should get a DNA test and find out if I'm related to Jack Willerton."

"You mean find out if you could be his daughter, Claire Ann, don't you?"

"Exactly. I've reached the point where I need to know one way or the other."

"Then, do it," Dr. Bentley told her. "However, if find out you are related, there are a lot of questions that you'll need answers to. For example, how did you wind up in the Patterson home and how did they manage to pass you off as their child?"

"And, if I'm not Claire Ann, then how can I explain my nightmares and her memories? No matter what I find out, I'll still be left with a million questions. And, Doctor, I doubt I'll ever get all the answers."

"Perhaps it is time to take that big step, Jessica. Get the test done and put your mind at ease."

"I guess," Jessica replied. "But, I'm afraid of what the results are going to be. The last thing I want to find out is that I'm the daughter of that monster. I don't know if I could handle finding out his blood flows through my veins."

"You can handle it. You're a strong woman. And, knowing is a lot healthier than not knowing. You asked for my advice, Jessica. I think you should get the test and deal with whatever the findings are."

"Easy for you to say, Doc," Jessica said.

"Not as easy as you may think," Dr. Bentley replied. "And, I am sorry, but I really do need to get home. Call me tomorrow if you need me."

Jessica pulled into her garage and shut off her car. "Thanks, Doc," she said and ended the call.

Jessica was sitting in a chair next to a child's play table, her knees practically reaching her chin. A little girl, dressed in a pretty yellow dress, was pouring her a cup of invisible tea.

"Sugar?" the little girl asked.

"Yes. Two lumps please," Jessica replied.

The little girl pretended to add the sugar to Jessica's tea and handed her the cup. Then, she sat down in a little chair across the table from Jessica.

"Be careful," she said. "It might be hot."

Jessica took a pretend sip and smacked her lips. "Perfect," she said.

The little girl smiled at Jessica. "Thank you. I take pride in making perfect tea for my guests."

Just as Jessica was to take another sip of tea, the little girl slapped her across the face, making

Jessica drop the cup of hot tea onto her lap.

Jessica cried out, "Why did you do that?"

The little girl slapped her again. "Stop it," Jessica yelled. "What's wrong with you?"

"You're not doing it right," the little girl exclaimed. "You're not following the clues. I want to go home and you're not helping me."

"I don't know what you want?" Jessica cried. "How can I help you leave?"

"Follow what I've told you. Tomorrow, when those men are in the woods, tell them where to find the bones."

"But, don't know where the bones are," Jessica said. "I don't know what you mean."

"Follow what I've told you," the girl said, again.

"Please, tell me again," Jessica begged.

The little girl, in the yellow dress, smiled. "Would you like some more tea?"

Jessica opened her eyes. The hum of the ceiling fan was the only noise in the room. She looked over at her bedroom window and realized it was still dark outside. The clock on her nightstand read 2:35 a.m. She moaned, rolled over, and within seconds she was sleeping again.

Five minutes later Jessica's eyes popped open and she sat up. "Oh, my god," she said. "It's the deer blind. She wants us to find the deer blind."

Chapter Thirty-two

"They were animal bones," Steve told Jessica.

"That was fast," she said.

"I know. They'll know more in a few days, but the examiner's best guess was some type of dog. With the tests they perform these days, they will be able to narrow it down to domestic or wild. Again, the examiner was guessing, but he figures they will be domestic. The bones have been out there a little less than a year."

"About the same time as when Jack Willerton was killed," Jessica remarked.

"Right. If I remember correctly, Willerton had a couple of dogs on his farm and they disappeared after he was killed."

"You remember correctly. CSI searched for them but didn't find them. They figured the dogs had run off. You think those bones could be from them?" Jessica asked Steve.

"Possible."

"Do you think the search today will turn up anything?" Peter asked.

"Never know. We may get lucky," Steve replied.

"The search team needs to look for a deer blind," Jessica said.

Steve looked over at her and then back at the road. "You think so?" he asked.

"I do," Jessica replied. "Do you think you could ask them to keep an eye out for a deer blind?"

Peter leaned forward in his seat. "They already found a couple of blinds out there."

Jessica turned her head, so she could see Peter who was sitting in the back of the car. "How do you know that?"

"I talked to Mac Littlefield last night. I called and asked what time they were starting the search this morning and he mentioned it."

"That's a strange thing to mention," Steve commented.

"It came up during our conversation," Peter told him. "We were talking about hunting and he mentioned the old blinds they had found during the search."

"What time are they starting today?" Steve asked.

"Well, it's daybreak, so I guess they're already out there."

Jessica turned back to the front and stared out the window. They were almost to the turn-off to the Willerton farm. She closed her eyes and enjoyed the quiet for a brief moment.

"The one they need to find has a shiny metal roof," she said, in a soft voice.

Steve glanced over at her, surprised at her comment. "What the hell? How do you know that?"

"I've seen it. I know it's crazy, but I've seen it in my dreams. Or, maybe when I was under hypnosis or had one of Claire Ann's memories. Whatever. There's a large clearing and the blind is set back into the woods. It has a metal roof, and when the sun is in just the right spot, it reflects off it. That's where the search team needs to go. They need to find that clearing."

"I might be able to help," Peter said, excitedly.

"Remember, I mentioned that I researched the Homestead Land Deeds, Jessica?"

"So?" she replied.

"It was the law that you had to clear the land, build a home, and live on the designated land. And, you had to farm it for at least five years."

"I remember you telling me that," Jessica said.

"Well, old Seth Willerton had multiple homestead deeds. After he cleared the area where the farm is today, he started clearing a second area."

"So, he cleared the land for his first and second claims. We know the farm was the first claim. Now we need to find out where the second 640 acres were," Steve declared.

"That's the thing. I know where they are," Peter said. "I flew over that area not too long ago. If we can get a plane up in the air, it won't take long to identify the location and get the coordinates."

"What do you think, Steve?" Jessica asked.

"I know someone," Steve replied.

Jessica grinned. "Of course, you do."

Steve, looking just a little smug, picked up his phone and called Detective Littlefield.

Twenty minutes later, Jessica, Steve, and Peter were at the farm, walking into the search team's tent. Mac Littlefield looked at the three of them as they entered, ended his call, and motioned for Steve to come closer to him.

"He agreed," Littlefield said, as Steve approached him. "He'll be in the air in fifteen minutes. You sure you know what you're talking about?"

"I'd like to say I'm one hundred percent, but I'm not. However, if we find what we're looking for, then all this won't be for nothing," Steve replied.

"You know, Steve," Littlefield whispered, "that Patterson woman could be a little nuts. I mean, here we are – searching through hundreds of acres trying to find a body that may not even be dead yet."

"She's not crazy," Steve responded. "And, remember, it was Judge Talaki that issued the order to search these woods. It wasn't Ms. Patterson."

"True. But it was all based on that crazy ass story that she told that judge."

"Well, Mac, we should know before the day is over, so let's just hang tight and wait for that chopper to do a flyover."

Peter felt his phone vibrate, walked outside the tent, and answered his call. He listened to the caller and nodded in agreement. "You're sure?" he asked, smiling at the information he had just received, and ended the call.

"Jessica," he called out.

She looked over at him, questioningly. He motioned for her to join him outside the tent.

"What's up?" she said, as she moved closer.

"They found Rachel's mother."

Chapter Thirty-three

"Has she been in Oregon this whole time?" Jessica asked Peter.

"It seems so. Her name is Nancy Fielding. She was a Carlton before she married Jack Willerton. She didn't divorce Jack, as she didn't want to let him know where she was. She just added the Fielding to her name," Peter told Jessica

"You know what that means, don't you?"

Peter suddenly realized what Jessica was referring to. "Oh, my god. She was still married to Willerton when he was murdered. She's the rightful owner of the property."

"You got that right," Jessica replied.

"Got what right?" Steve said as he walked over to where they were talking.

"We just found out Rachel's mother is living in Oregon," Peter told him. "It seems she was still married to Willerton when he was killed, so she owns all of this property."

Steve looked surprised. "He didn't leave a will?"

"Not that we could find," Jessica replied.

"Well, there you go," Steve said.

"What?" Peter asked.

"The motive for killing Willerton. You just found your motive."

"You think Rachel's mother came back here and murdered him after all these years?" Jessica asked. "That's a little out there, don't you think?"

"She could have hired someone to do it."

"Why now?" Jessica questioned.

"Just saying," Steve replied and looked up at the sky. "Hear that? The chopper is here."

They heard the chopper before they saw it passing over them. It banked to the left and circled back the way it had come.

"That was fast," Peter said.

"It doesn't take long to find what you're looking for when you're up there," Steve said. "I'll go check with Littlefield." As he started to walk back towards the tent, Jessica called to him, asking him to wait. "We're coming with you," she said.

Three hours later, Peter stood up and stretched his body. "This waiting is for the birds," he remarked. "I'm bored and I'm hungry. I think I'll drive into Millstone and get something to eat. You wanna come with?"

Jessica looked up at him and smiled. "No. I think I'll stay here. I figure, if I leave, they'll find something and I'll miss it."

Peter grinned. "So, you want to be here when they announce the big find, do you?"

"Don't tease me, Peter. I'm a nervous wreck. The very idea that this could come to nothing terrifies me. Just look at the expense involved here. I'll be the laughingstock of Iron Mountain."

"Don't get ahead of yourself, Jessica. There are still about six hours of daylight left. You never know what might happen."

Jessica sighed deeply. "I guess, but it's so nerve-racking."

"Look at the bright side. If they do find a body

close to a deer blind, you'll have every nut in the Iron Mountain area knocking on your door asking you to relay a message to some dead relative. Hell, they'd probably come from all over the world. You could start a whole new business. You'll be rich and famous."

"I don't think that's funny," Jessica told him, as she held back a grin.

Peter laughed. "Yes, you do. So, do you want me to bring you something to eat?"

"You know there's food in the tent, don't you?" Jessica commented.

"I need to get away from here for a little while," Peter said. "Besides, those sandwiches don't look that appetizing."

"How about you surprise me? I don't know what fast food places are in Millstone, so you pick one. But whatever you get – no onions for me."

"Got it," Peter told her. "I'll be back soon." He walked towards the car, whistling.

Jessica watched as he drove away. She smiled to herself, thinking how glad she was that she had gotten to know him. And, how glad she was that he had such a great brother.

By three o'clock, Jessica's butt was sore from sitting most of the day and she decided to walk over to the barn. She knew she wouldn't find anything new there, but she needed some exercise. Peter declined the invitation to join her, so she took off towards the barn by herself. She was about halfway there when Peter yelled her name.

She turned and saw Peter motioning to her to

come back. "What's up?" she yelled.

"They found something," he shouted to her. "Come back."

Jessica ran back to where Peter was standing. "What?" she exclaimed. "What did they find?"

"I'm not sure. I heard Mac Littlefield talking on his radio. He told someone not to disturb anything until the coroner was called out. He said to tape off the area and wait."

A cold shiver ran through Jessica's body and she felt goosebumps on her arms. She started to shake uncontrollably and dropped down to her knees. "Ohhhhh," she cried out. She moaned again and took deep breaths, as the shaking gradually ended. Tears filled her eyes and she looked up at Peter.

"She's gone," she whispered.

Peter bent down and took Jessica by the arms and helped her up. "Are you okay? My god, Jessica, you scared the crap out of me."

Jessica took another deep breath, closed her eyes, and expelled the air in an effort to calm herself. "She's gone, Peter. Claire Ann is gone."

"What do you mean, she's gone?"

"I don't know how to explain it. My whole body felt tight – like I was being pulled inside myself - and then total release. It was like a small explosion happened inside of me. It had to be Claire Ann leaving me. Her spirit is free." Jessica started to sob, tears running down her cheeks.

Peter took her in his arms and held her as she cried. After a few moments, Jessica backed away and laughed nervously. "I'm sorry," she told Peter. "I don't know what came over me."

"You have nothing to be sorry for."

"You must think I'm really crazy," Jessica said.

Peter met her gaze and smiled gently at her. "I know what I just saw, and I certainly don't think you're crazy. I believe you when you tell me Claire Ann just said goodbye.

"They found her, you know," Jessica uttered. "They found her body out there in those woods. She's been alone out there for over twenty-five years, Peter."

"I know," Peter said.

"Now her soul can rest in peace."

"Amen to that," whispered Peter.

"I'm not Claire Ann."

"No, you're not," Peter agreed.

Jessica glanced over at a commotion by the tent. "Some of the guys from the search party are back," she said.

"Let's go see what they found." Steve looked at the men coming out of the woods and saw his brother heading toward them. "Steve's here," he told Jessica.

Jessica smiled, as Steve approached them, glad to see him. She immediately realized by the look on Steve's face that he was upset. "What is it?" she asked, as he reached them. "What's wrong? You found her, didn't you?"

"We found the blind, Jessica. It was just where you said it would be, close to a large clearing. It wasn't standing any longer, but most of the pieces were still there, including a tin roof."

"For god's sake, Steve, did you find her body?"

"We found a body. I can't say for sure that it's

the Willington girl. It's too soon. The remains were under gobs of debris that had accumulated over the years. Some of the clothes were still recognizable and from what I saw they were girl clothes. With the body being covered up all those years, with leaves and pine needles and that metal roof – well, it was like a burial site. As I said, we can't call it yet, but I'm pretty sure it's going to be Claire Ann that we found."

"It was," Jessica said. "It was her."

"How can you be so sure?" Steve asked her.

"Because, she's gone."

Steve looked over at his brother, a questioning look on his face. "Peter?"

"Trust me, Steve. Jessica knows. But something is bothering you. I can tell by the way you're acting."

"We found two bodies, Peter."

Jessica stared at Steve, unbelieving what she had just heard. "What do you mean, you found two bodies? There was someone in that deer blind with Claire Ann?"

"No. Not even close to where she was found. The men that headed west this morning found bones scattered over a large area. They haven't found a skull but there's no question that the bones are human. It's going to take a while and it won't be easy, but we're hoping we can get a match to a missing person."

"God, will this ever end," Jessica cried out. "Do they have any idea of how long they've been there? Are they male or female?"

"Jessica, slow down a little," Steve replied, "They just found them. I don't have the answers. In fact, we may never know for sure who it is."

"But they identified that Williams boy. Won't they be able to do the same thing with these bones?" Peter asked his brother.

"It depends. They got lucky with the Williams kid. They managed to extract enough bone marrow to do a DNA test. The condition of these bones is worse, plus we haven't found the skull, so there's no way to do a dental match. We'll have to wait and see. The County Coroner has been called, and he's already contacted a forensics anthropologist," Steve told them.

"Will they extend the search?" Jessica asked.

"Mac's calling it quits for today," Steve said. "The two days are up, but I'm pretty sure the search will be extended until the entire property has been gone over. Finding one body was bad, but finding three could be an indication that these woods were used as a dumping ground."

"I doubt there are any more bodies out there," Jessica said. "Claire Ann and her brother died in 1990. Ted Williams was collateral damage. I seriously don't think Willerton Woods was used for a dumping ground."

"You're probably right," Steve agreed. "But I think Littlefield is going to turn those woods upside down to be sure.

Jessica turned and glanced over at the hill where the cemetery was. "Of course," she said, "there's always a possibility that there are more empty coffins buried up there. Only God only knows where those bodies might be."

Chapter Thirty-four

"I don't need a mother! I can take care of myself!" Rachel yelled. "The judge is gonna emancipate me. Tell my mother to go the hell back to where she came from."

"You need to talk to her. Everything has changed now. She's the legal recipient of your father's estate. You get nothing unless she decides to give it to you. Do you understand?"

Rachel glared at Jessica. "It's not fair! I'm the one who put up with all his crap. I'm the one he molested for six years. She ran off and enjoyed her life after leaving me behind to be abused by him. Well, you can tell her to go fuck herself, Jessica."

Jessica and Peter looked at each other. Peter shrugged. "Not much we can do about it. If she doesn't want to see her, she doesn't have to see her," he said. "Although, Rachel, there's something you should know."

Rachel threw him a dirty look. "And, what's that Mr. Big Shot Attorney?"

"Just remember that this big shot attorney and Ms. Patterson are the ones who got you off. That's the only reason you're not in jail right now."

"Bullshit," Rachel retorted. "It's because the State didn't have enough evidence. And, you know it. So, don't give me that 'I'm your savior shit', Peter."

"Stop it, Rachel, and listen. You are not going to be emancipated," Jessica brusquely told her. "The judge ruled against it when he was informed that your mother is alive and on her way to Michigan. Your choices are either live with a foster family until you're eighteen or live with your mother."

Rachel looked like she'd just been slapped in the face. "That's not true. What you just said. That can't be true."

"It's true, all right. So, you need to pick one – foster home or your mother," Peter told her.

"But, how could the judge do that? She left me. How can he make me live with a woman that deserted me? It's not fair," Rachel whined. "That money should be mine."

"It may not be fair, but that's the way it is," Jessica said. "Maybe, you could come to some kind of an agreement with her. She doesn't want to stay here. Her home is in Oregon and she wants to go back there."

Rachel got up from the table they were sitting at and started pacing. "I won't do it," she cried out. "I'm not moving to Oregon."

"Perhaps, you could stay with your aunt. Maybe, your mother could pay her to take care of you until your eighteen. That way, you could be with your friends. You wouldn't have to change schools and you could graduate here." Peter suggested.

"That's a great idea, Peter," Jessica said. "Rachel, you'd be with people who love you. What do you think about that idea?"

"My aunt doesn't love me. If she did, I'd be living with her already.

"That's not true. You know she's been ill and couldn't take on the responsibility of taking care of you. But, she's better now. I'm sure she and your uncle would be happy to do it. What do you say, Rachel? Should we see if we can work this out? Will you meet with your mother?"

Rachel didn't say anything for a few moments. "I'll do it if my mother promises to give me some money when I turn eighteen," she said, smiling. "Although, I should rightfully get all of it," she added.

"So, should we let her know you'll see her?" Jessica asked her.

"I guess. If I really have to."

"You have to," Peter told her.

"Fine," Rachel said. "But, before I see her, you have to make sure that she agrees to this."

After two hours of yelling insults, dozens of 'I'm so sorry', and buckets of tears, Rachel and her mother were now acting like the best of friends. They had hugged each other and, now, sitting at a table in the conference room, they were holding hands.

After playing referee between Rachel and her mom for almost the entire two hours, Jessica was exhausted. And, hungry. "Would you like to order lunch before we finalize the arrangements?" she asked.

"I know I could eat," Peter replied.

"I could go for something," Nancy Fielding told them. "How about you, Rachel?" she asked her daughter.

"Pizza. I want pizza," Rachel replied.

"I don't eat meat," Nancy stated. "Perhaps, we could do half meat and half cheese."

"I'll order two," Peter said. "One of each."

"Sounds good," Jessica said. "So, Nancy, what's

it like living near the ocean?" she asked, changing the topic.

"It's wonderful. I'm just sorry that Rachel doesn't want to go back with me." She looked at her daughter and said, "I would love you to change your mind. But, if you're dead set on staying here, I hope you'll come and visit me sometime. I'll bet you that you'll change your mind, once you see how beautiful it is where I live, and want to stay."

Rachel smiled at her. "I might visit you, but I doubt I'd stay. I like it here and I've got friends here."

"And, relatives, don't forget," Jessica added.

"How could I forget when I'm going to live with Aunt Joyce and Uncle Bob?" Rachel exclaimed. "I wish Jillian was still here. We used to have so much fun together."

"When was the last time you saw Jillian?" Nancy asked.

"A little over a year. . . No, wait. I meant it's been a long time. Maybe, four or five years."

Jessica didn't miss the bump. She remembered that Rachel had told her, before the trial, that she hadn't seen her cousin for four years, but, just now, she had started to tell her mother that it had been a year. She stared at Rachel and realized that, except for the slight blushing of her cheeks, she showed no signs of lying.

"Pizza's on its way," Peter said, as he ended his phone call to Marco's Pizza. "It'll be here in about half an hour or so. Whataya say we finish this up, so we can draw up the final arrangements and present it to the judge in the morning. Nancy, did you make your sister aware that she would probably have to appear before the judge?"

"I did. No problem. Whatever you need for Rachel to be in a nice, safe environment, she's ready to do," Nancy told him.

"Good. The sooner we get this done, the sooner Rachel will be out of that foster home," Peter told her.

"My sister said she doesn't want any money for Rachel's upkeep," Nancy informed him. "Did I mention that?"

"No. But, that will certainly make points with the judge. He'll like the idea that she's doing it because Rachel is family and not because she's going to be paid," Peter said.

"Of course, Rachel, I'll be sending you money every month. You know, for clothes and stuff. What you don't spend you can put away for college," Nancy stated.

"Which you are paying for? Right?" Rachel said.

"Of course. It's part of our agreement," Nancy said, locking eyes with Rachel.

"Right," Rachel agreed. "It is." She glanced over at Jessica and asked, "If the judge approves all of this, when will I be able to go to my aunt's house?"

"Immediately," Jessica said.

"There's one thing I'd like you to do before you go back to Oregon," Rachel said, looking at her mother.

"Of course, dear. Anything. What is it?" Nancy asked.

"I want you to drive out to the farm with me, so I can get some of my things. I didn't think going out there by myself would bother me, but it does. I'd like you to be with me. Besides, wouldn't you like to see the farm one more time?"

Nancy looked surprised. "I'm not sure if that's a good idea, Rachel, after what happened there and all. If there's anything you need, maybe we can get someone to pick it up for you. I am not comfortable with the idea of going back there."

Rachel smirked. "Why not? Too many bad memories?"

Nancy, suddenly flustered, turned away. "Of course, there are bad memories. I would think you have enough of them, also, to keep you from wanting to go back there."

"Oh, I do. But it could be the last time I ever go back there and I'd really like you to come with me. Please. I think that's the least you can do for me."

"I guess we could go out there if we don't hang around too long. You promise you'll just get what you want and we can leave right away?"

Rachel smiled at her. "Of course. It won't take but a minute or two."

"All right, then. I guess we can do that before I go back to Oregon," Nancy said, trying to hide the fact that she was totally shaken up by Rachel's request.

Chapter Thirty-five

Judge Talaki signed the petition, which allowed Rachel to reside with her Aunt Joyce and Uncle Bob until she was eighteen. Rachel had called Jessica a few days later, thanking her for her help. She told Jessica that her mother was staying for a few more days and then she was heading back to Oregon.

When Jessica asked Rachel how things were going between the two of them, Rachel had hesitated and, then, simply replied that things were okay. She told Jessica that they still had to go out to the farm, so she could get her stuff.

The search was over at Willerton Woods, and no more remains had been discovered. The open graves had been filled in, and the farm was now deserted. The only sound to be heard was the wind whispering through the trees.

Rachel was sitting in Dr. Bentley's office. This was her third visit in a week, and Dr. Bentley had just informed her that he didn't feel it necessary for her to continue her sessions with him.

"Really?" she said. "You think I'm cured?"

Dr. Bentley smiled. "It's not a matter of being cured, Jessica. You haven't had a bad dream or a nightmare since the remains of Claire Ann were found. You told me that you felt her leave your body and that she was gone. So, unless your nightmares come back, I don't see any reason to continue."

"But we haven't solved the puzzle," Jessica exclaimed. "I still don't know why she was with me to begin with. Why me? I mean, why did she choose me?"

Jessica smiled as Dr. Bentley reached for his pipe. "It's think time," she commented.

He looked confused. "Excuse me," he said.

"You always play with your pipe when you are thinking about what you are going to say next. You just reached for your pipe so, I figure you're thinking about your answer."

"Did you follow through and get a DNA test?" he asked Jessica, ignoring her comments about his pipe.

"I did. But, what difference does that make now?"

"It wouldn't surprise me if you find out that you and Claire Ann are related in some fashion. When the settlers purchased land through the Homestead Act, relatives tried to stay close to each other. I think there's a good possibility that your parents' relatives settled close to the Willertons. You could be distant cousins or something."

"You think that Claire Ann picked me because I'm related to her?" Jessica asked. "That's a little farfetched. Why didn't she choose Rachel? After all, they are sisters."

"I'm just throwing it out there. Do you have a better idea?" Dr. Bentley inquired.

Jessica sighed. "Not really. I guess I'll never know the answer to 'why me'."

"Claire Ann was murdered and left to rot in those woods," Dr. Bentley said. "There are. . .."

"We think it's Claire Ann," Jessica replied, correcting him.

"Let me finish. Some people believe that a

spiritual possession is a phenomenon in which a stray being, from the spirit world, possesses a person living on earth. This possession can be constant or temporary. Most of these spirits are known as 'evil spirits' but that doesn't mean they are harmful. Usually, there is an issue that was not settled before they died and they want it taken care of. The only avenue these spirits have to 'fix it' is to enter a living being and take over until the issue is settled."

"Do you believe this?" Jessica asked.

"I do and I don't. Modern medicine and the science world don't recognize the existence of spiritual possession. So, my training says no. However, when I have a patient, like you, it's hard to discredit it. I guess you could say I'm in the middle when it comes to this subject."

"Well, as far as I'm concerned, she was here and now she's not. I guess I lean towards the believing side of it."

"I don't think we'll have the answers in our lifetime, Jessica."

"I kind of miss her," Jessica admitted to Dr. Bentley. "I know that's probably a strange thing to say. But she was with me for such a long time and it feels different without her. I actually feel smaller. . . No, that's not the right word. I feel lighter. Does that make sense?"

"It does. So, what now for Jessica?"

Jessica smiled. "The same as always. I'll keep trying to right the injustices in the world. Not always exciting but certainly fulfilling."

"I expect you to keep me up to date. Call me if

you need to talk."

"I'll do that, Doctor," Jessica said. She picked up her purse and headed towards the door. As she was about to leave, she turned and looked at Dr. Bentley. "Thank you, for everything," she said, smiling. "I sincerely mean it."

"You're welcome, Jessica. And, good luck."

Chapter Thirty-six

Jessica was at her desk trying to concentrate on the file in front of her. Her thoughts, however, kept returning to what Dr. Bentley had said at their last session. The thought that she might be related to the Willertons was a little disturbing. Yet, she was curious to find out and wished that the DNA test results would be ready soon.

She jumped when her phone rang, laughed at herself for being so jumpy, and answered her phone.

"Jessica Patterson," she said.

"It's Peter, Jessica. I just received a copy of the County Coroner's report. Did you get a copy?"

"No, I haven't. When did you get it?"

"Just a few minutes ago," Peter said.

"Is it Claire Ann?" she asked.

"It is a young girl that they found. They determined that the remains have been in those woods for at least twenty-five or more years. They can't, however, say that it is definitely Claire Ann Willerton."

"Why the hell not?" Jessica yelled.

"Just wait a minute before you go all ballistic. Claire Ann's existence was almost unknown. She wasn't even six years old when she died. She had never attended school. No one ever reported her missing. Remember, Jessica, that we determined her mother died around the same time, although we can't prove it. Jack Willerton told everyone that his wife had run off with their two kids. Nobody missed her and basically, no one cared."

"For crying out loud, Peter, you know it's her."

"I know it and you know it. But, as far as the coroner is concerned, it is an unknown. They can say, however, that she is Jack Willerton's daughter."

"Well, if they're sure about that, and he didn't have any other daughters at that time, why won't they say it's Claire Ann?"

"They can't speculate. You know that. They have nothing to compare the remains to, so that's the best they can do."

"What about the other body they found? Have they identified that one yet?"

"Are you sitting down?" Peter asked.

"I am. And, I get a feeling that what you're about to tell me isn't going to be good."

"They've identified it."

"What the hell, Peter? Just tell me who it is," Jessica yelled.

"It's Jillian Wickstrom."

Jessica's heart started to pound and she felt light-headed for a few seconds. She took a deep breath and let it out.

"Jessica? Are you still there?"

"Are they sure?" Jessica said softly.

"They're sure. Dental records confirmed it."

"Well, shit!" Jessica exclaimed. "I sure didn't see that coming. Wait a minute. The last I heard they hadn't found a skull."

"It was found the next day. At least, part of it was. There still enough teeth attached to the upper jaw to get a match."

"No one told me," Jessica said, obviously upset. "How come you know about it?"

"I hear things."

"Well, the next time you hear things that I might be interested in, please let me know," Jessica remarked, indignantly.

"I'm sorry I didn't call and tell you."

"Forget it. Has Rachel's aunt been informed?"

"The police are on their way to the Wickstrom home right now to inform her parents. I wouldn't wish that job on anyone."

"This will be hard on Rachel, too. She said that Jillian and she were really close a few years back," Jessica said.

"It looks like both Ted Williams and Jillian Wickstrom were killed on the same day. It's interesting, though, that their bodies were found in opposite directions from each other."

"Do you know how she died?" Jessica asked Peter.

"They figure the weapon was a shotgun, just like Williams."

"I imagine the same person killed both of them," Jessica observed.

"You know what it looks like to me, Jessica? I think that Jillian Wickstrom, Ted Williams, and an unknown third person killed Jack Willerton and cut him up with a chainsaw. And, I think that the third person knew Wickstrom and Williams really well. Might even have been related to one of them."

"You think Rachel killed them?"

"I do. I've always believed she had something to do with it. I know - it's just a theory - but that's what I believe happened."

"Well, if it is, we helped a cold-blooded killer go free," Jessica declared.

"I'm not taking the blame for that," Peter told her. "The D.A. prosecuted the case way too soon, and the judge let her go. It's the system – not me or you."

"If Rachel is a killer, then we're all to blame, Peter."

"You know, I was happy doing civil cases. I never imagined I'd be involved in working on a case with you. It's funny how things turn out, isn't it?"

"I had my doubts about you when this started, Peter, but not anymore. You've turned out to be one fine attorney and I'm proud to have been part of your team. More than that, though, I'm proud to have you as a friend."

"Thank you, Jessica, that means a lot to me. I like being your friend. Hey, who knows? Some day you could be my sister-in-law."

Jessica laughed. "Let's not even go there. I've got to go, Peter. I'll talk to you later."

As soon as she hung up, Jessica's phone rang. "Jessica Patterson," she answered.

"Ms. Patterson, this is Barb from Central DNA Testing calling. We have the results of your DNA tests. Can you verify your name, address, and the last four numbers of your social security card for me?"

Chapter Thirty-seven

Peter Fisher was in his office, working on a case he hoped would be settled out of court. He considered it frivolous and a waste of time, but these petty cases were what paid the bills. His client, Mr. Simpson was suing his neighbor, Mr. Prite, claiming Mr. Prite's dog, Ginger, had dug up his garden, ruining his prize-winning gladiolas. He wanted restitution for the plants, plus compensation for his pain and suffering.

Peter sat back in his chair and sighed. It had only been a few days since he had last seen Jessica, and he was missing her. He had gotten used to being around her and was starting to wonder if he had feelings for her. Well, that ship sailed, he thought, when I introduced her to Steve. Too late, now.

He swung his chair around and turned on his police scanner, which was sitting on a table behind his desk. He sat back and listened to the police calls being broadcasted over the scanner. He loved doing this, and, at times, he wished he had become a cop like his brother, Steve. But, then, when he heard the gory details about some innocent victim or a cop that had been shot, he was more than satisfied with his chosen profession.

His thoughts strayed back to Jessica and he picked up his phone and called her.

"Jessica Patterson," she answered.

"It's me. Peter."

"Morning. What's up?" Jessica asked.

"How about lunch?"

Jessica hesitated. "I don't know if today is good

for me, Peter. I'm pretty busy."

"You need to eat, don't you?" Peter said.

"I was planning on ordering in," Jessica said.

"How about I pick up something from Madder's Deli and bring it over? We can eat in your office."

"That sounds okay. Let's do that."

"Is twelve okay?" Peter asked.

"Works for me. I'll see you then," Jessica said and ended the call.

Peter sat back in his chair and closed his eyes. He wondered if Jessica liked club sandwiches. Madder's made a fantastic one, loaded with gobs of bacon and turkey. He considered getting a couple of them for lunch, and some curly fries. He realized that, even though they had spent over a year working together, he still knew very little about her.

He had turned the volume down on the scanner, so he wasn't sure if he had heard right when the name Willerton was mentioned. He reached over, increased the volume on the scanner, and listened intently. An APB was being reported for Rachel Willerton, seventeen years old, who was last seen on Tuesday, at the County Mall in Iron Mountain. She had been wearing blue jeans and a yellow top. She was believed to have been in the company of two males, possibly in their late teens to early twenties. Anyone, with any information, was asked to notify the Iron Mountain Police Department.

He picked up his phone and called Jessica.

"Jessica Patterson."

"It's me, again," Peter said. "Rachel is missing. I just heard it over my police scanner. I figured you'd want to know."

"You have a police scanner?" Jessica asked.

"Did you hear what I just said?" Peter replied. "Rachel is missing."

"I'm sorry, I heard the words police scanner, but your phone is cracking up. Did you say Rachel is missing?"

"Yes. She's been missing since Tuesday."

"That's over seventy-two hours," Jessica commented. "That's not good."

"She was last seen with two guys at the County Mall."

"That poor Wickstrom woman hasn't even had a chance to bury her daughter and now this shit. Rachel's mother is back in Oregon, right?" Jessica asked.

"I think she left on Monday. I'm not a hundred percent sure about that, though. I know she wanted to spend a few days with her sister and Rachel before she left, and then she was heading back home. I'm pretty sure she left on Monday."

"I wonder if she and Rachel ever made it out to the farm. Rachel said she wanted to get a few . . .. Oh, my god. I bet she's there. I'll bet you anything Rachel went back to the farm."

"You may be right. I'm going to call the police and ask them if they've checked there," Peter said.

"Call me back and let me know what you find out," Jessica said.

"I will. And, then I'm coming over to your office."

"It's too early for lunch," Jessica told him.

"I'll bring a couple of cappuccinos and some

muffins. We'll have a late breakfast."

Peter called Jessica on his car phone as he drove to her office. Her line was busy, so he told the receptionist to tell her he was on his way.

He didn't bother to stop for muffins or cappuccinos.

Jessica was standing, looking out her office window when Peter walked in.

She turned towards him and shook her head. "I can't figure this out," she said. "Why would Rachel take off like this?"

"She may have been abducted," Peter said. "They are pulling the surveillance videos from the mall and checking them now. There's a possibility that the two men she was with took her."

"She should have been in school," Jessica stated. "Why wasn't she in school?"

"School's out for the summer, Jessica," Peter reminded her.

"Oh, ya. That's right. Then, why wasn't her aunt watching her?"

"She's seventeen. Remember? She doesn't need a babysitter," Peter said.

Jessica plopped down into her office chair and sighed. "I know. It's just that I feel responsible for her. She's had a rough life and she needs to get her head straightened out."

"Well, you're not responsible for her and neither am I. We were just her attorneys. We did our job and we should put all this behind us."

"I found out that I'm related to her," Jessica told Peter. "My DNA test showed that we are some kind of shirttail relatives. I haven't quite determined how, yet."

Peter looked concerned. "Are you okay? I know that the last thing you wanted was for that test to come back with those results."

Jessica shrugged. "Not much I can do about it now. We can't pick and choose who we want for our relatives."

"It makes more sense now, though, doesn't it?" Peter said.

"What's that?"

"The whole thing with Claire Ann and all. It looks like she picked you because she was related to you."

"I guess," she said. She looked him up and down, checking him out, and frowned.

"What?" Peter said, feeling uncomfortable.

"Where the hell is my cappuccino?"

Chapter Thirty-eight

Peter called Jessica around five. "I wonder if I can drop by again. I have some news about Rachel that I'm sure you going to want to hear. I can be there by six."

"I'd really like to get out of here," Jessica said. "It's been a long day and I just want to go home and relax."

"You're going to want to hear this, Jessica. You should know about it before it breaks on the ten o'clock news."

"Just tell me now," she said, impatiently. "What the hell is so important that you have to tell me in person?"

"I'd rather you hear it from Steve. I called him and asked him to meet me at your office. He's on his way and should be there within the hour."

"Fine," she had replied. "Just don't be late. I'm tired, hungry, and crabby."

"No shit," Peter said. "You could have fooled me."

It was a little after six, Steve had just arrived from Marinette, and Peter had just called again, telling her he would be there in a few minutes.

Steve looked around Jessica's office and smiled. "Nice digs," he observed. He walked over to her office window and looked out over the town. "Good view, too," he added.

"Thanks. I enjoy it," Jessica told him. "But, why are you here? Not that I don't enjoy seeing you, because I do. In fact, you being here is the highlight of my day."

"Actually, Jessica, it was Peter who asked me to come up and see you."

"I know. He told me," Jessica replied.

"It's been a couple of days since Rachel Willerton went missing and Pete asked me if I could find out what's going on. I checked with Mac Littlefield – you remember him, don't you?"

"Of course. He led up the search team out at the Willerton farm."

"Anyway, he filled me in on what's going on and Peter thought it might be better if you heard it from me. You know, first hand."

Jessica looked puzzled. "Heard what from you? What's going on, Steve? You're scaring me."

"Sorry. There's nothing for you to be afraid of. However, I'd like to wait until Peter gets here if that's okay?" He glanced around her office. "You wouldn't happen to have some coffee, would you?" he asked her.

"No, I don't have any coffee," she exclaimed. "Everything's been cleaned up and put away for the night. Just tell me why you're here, would you?"

"Show me where to go and I'll put a pot on. I could use some coffee."

Jessica, frustrated and wondering what the hell was going on, pointed toward her office door. "There's a kitchen out the door and to your left," she snapped at him.

"A kitchen, huh? Nice. I'll be right back," Steve said.

Jessica watched him walk into the adjoining

area and waited. A few moments later she heard voices and realized that Peter must have arrived and was talking to his brother. She started to join them, thought better of it, and sat down behind her desk. Five minutes later, Steve came into her office, carrying two cups of coffee, followed by Peter.

Steve handed Jessica a cup and sat down in a chair across from her. "Light with no sugar, if I remembered right."

"Thank you." She glanced over at Peter, who was standing in the room, looking at her. "So, Peter, here we all are. Perhaps, now, you and your brother would clue me in as to what is going on. What's the big mystery?"

"Steve?" Peter prompted.

Steve took a sip of his coffee. "Hot," he said.

"I imagine it is, seeing as how you just made it," Jessica replied.

"Jessica, I'm here because Pete feels that you might be a little fragile right now, with everything that you've gone through lately. I don't know if that's the case, but I respect Pete and, well. . . I care about you and I . . . "

"Just fucking say it, will you?" Jessica said, raising her voice.

Steve looked her in the eyes. "Nancy Fielding is dead," Steve said, softly. "Her body was found out at the Willerton farm a few hours ago."

Jessica shook her head, in disbelief. "No," she whispered. "That can't be right. She's in Oregon." She turned to Peter and said, "You told me she went back to Oregon on Monday."

"The coroner determined she was murdered sometime on Monday. Due to the condition of the body, it's a little hard to pin down the exact time, but it definitely was on Monday."

"But I thought she was going back to Oregon on Monday."

"She was," Steve said. "Rachel was going to take her to the airport after they stopped at the farm."

"Did Rachel kill her?" Jessica asked.

"Detective Littlefield figures she was in on it. He doesn't think she could have done it by herself. She had to have had help."

"The two boys she was with at the Mall," Jessica stated.

"Most likely," Steve said.

"How did she die? Was she shot?"

Steve looked down at his hands and was quiet.

"Steve?"

He looked up at her and shook his head no.

"I need to know how she died," Jessica said. "I'll find out eventually, so you might as well tell me.

"Tell her, Steve," Peter said. "She's right. She'll find out anyway."

"Mac Littlefield's best guess is that Rachel's two friends were waiting in the house when Rachel and her mom got there. We can't tell if she put up much of a fight, but I doubt it. She's a. . . she was a small woman, probably didn't weigh more than 115 pounds. They tore her clothes off and tied her to the bed. I mean that literally. Her clothes were in shreds. Most likely, Rachel watched as her two friends raped her mother repeatedly."

"How do you know that Rachel was part of it?" Jessica asked.

"Let me finish," Steve said. "Then, they tortured her. She had cigarette burns over her entire body, but mostly on her breasts and in the vaginal area." Steve looked at Jessica, who had turned pale and looked like she was going to be ill. He turned to Peter and said, "I knew this was a bad idea."

"No!" Jessica yelled. "I want to hear it. All of it."

Steve sighed. "Are you sure? It gets worse, Jessica."

"Go on,' she demanded.

"Littlefield figures she was raped and tortured for hours. She had superficial cuts on her face, her arms, and her legs. Her torso got the worst of it. The words 'bitch mom' were carved on it and the cuts there were a lot deeper."

"Are you sure she was alive the whole time?" Jessica asked, her voice hardly audible.

"There's no doubt she was, due to the amount of blood on the scene. If she had been dead when they cut her, there would have been a lot less blood."

"What killed her?"

Steve hesitated. He picked up his coffee cup and stood up. "I'll be right back. I'm gonna get some more coffee. You want more?"

Jessica shook her head no. "I'm fine, thanks."

"Peter? You want more?"

Peter looked at him. "I don't think so. Thanks."

As Steve walked out of the room, Jessica glanced over at Peter. "Are you okay, Peter?" she asked him. "You don't look so good,"

"This is one of the reasons I didn't become a cop," he told her. "I don't know how those guys can deal with shit like this."

"You want to hear something?"

"What's that?" Peter replied.

"I used to wonder what it would be like to hurt somebody bad. Even kill them. I used to almost get off thinking about it. But, ever since this case, for some reason, that's changed. Stuff like this – hearing what happened to Rachel's mom – makes me ill. Ever since they found Claire Ann's body, I feel different. It's almost like I'm a different person."

"It's probably because this case has been so personal. And, you have changed a lot since I first met you."

She glanced up at him. "You think so?"

"I do. You aren't the same tough person you were when we started working together. You were a ballbuster, for sure. You may still be tough, Jessica, but there's a softer side of you that's come through. I like that person."

Jessica smiled at him. "Thank you, Peter. That means a lot to me."

Steve walked back into Jessica's office. "How about we finish this up and go to dinner?"

Jessica smiled at him. "I'm not sure I'll want to eat after this. Are you staying in town tonight?"

"I'm staying with Pete. I'll go back to Marinette tomorrow." Steve got comfortable, took a sip of coffee, and set the cup on Jessica's desk. "Her throat was cut. That's how she died. She bled out, lying in that rotten cabin, in the same filthy bed where her daughter was molested for six years by her father."

"Do they know where Rachel is?" Jessica inquired. "She was seen on Tuesday at the Mall, so, obviously, she didn't run off."

"I'm sorry, but she's dead, too, Jessica."

Jessica's head jerked up, shocked by what she had just heard. She looked at Steve's face and realized how hard telling her this had been.

"How?" Jessica whispered.

"They found her hanging from a rafter in the barn. It looks like she killed herself."

"The same rafter where her father was found?" Jessica asked.

"The same one," Steve said.

"Suicide?" she asked.

"That's what it looks like," Steve replied.

"I don't believe it. Rachel wasn't the kind of person who would kill herself."

"Well, the evidence points that she did, including a note she left. She climbed up a ladder, put a rope around her neck, and kicked the ladder out from under herself. The fall broke her neck. I guess you could say, in a way, she was lucky."

"Lucky? She's dead. I don't call that lucky," Jessica said.

"She would have spent the rest of her life in jail or gotten the death penalty."

"That poor child never had a chance. What did the note say?" Jessica inquired.

"She said to tell her aunt and uncle that she was sorry about what happened to Jillian and that she wanted them to have her farm."

"It almost sounds like a confession," Peter stated.

"Perhaps. I guess we'll never know for sure," Steve said.

"How long before this story breaks?" Peter asked his brother, steering the conversation in a new direction.

"I imagine it will be on the late news," Steve told him. "You know how hard it is to keep something like this quiet. By the way, Pete, it was your call to Detective Littlefield that made them check out at the farm. Otherwise, they might still be looking for Rachel."

"It was Jessica's idea. I just made the call," Peter said.

"Have they found the two boys she was with?" Jessica asked.

"Nope. Funny thing, about that. The car they were driving is still at the farm. Forensics is going over it right now, looking for prints."

"They probably took the car Rachel was using to drive her mother to the airport," Peter said.

"Nope. That car belongs to her aunt. It's still at the farm, too," Steve told him.

"That doesn't make any sense," Jessica said. "Why walk away when two cars are sitting there? Unless, of course, there was a third person that picked them up."

"That's a possibility, but . . . ."

"Oh, crap!" Jessica cried out.

"What?" Peter asked.

"Willerton Woods!"

228

"What about Willerton Woods?" Peter asked.

"I'll bet you both a dinner that Mac Littlefield and his team will be searching Willerton Woods one more time," she declared.

Steve took a sip of his coffee. "Pete, you wanna take that bet?" he asked, as he put the cup back on Jessica's desk.

Peter shook his head. "Not in a million years."

About the Author

I was born in Idaho in 1939. My father's job demanded that we frequently move so, by the age of ten, I had lived in Idaho, Montana, Colorado, Michigan, and finally Wisconsin.

I am the proud mother of three wonderful sons and two fantastic grandsons. I have no plans to acquire another husband, as they are just too much work.

For most of my life, I worked as an accountant. Two years before I retired, I did a complete switch in careers and managed two Curves fitness facilities in Illinois. I retired in 2002 and moved to Branson, MO. In 2012, I moved to Indiana to be closer to my family and have resided in Highland since then.

I enjoy a good laugh and figure it's my sense of humor that has kept me going when times were tough. Reading has always been one of my passions and I still read a couple of books a week.

Most of my life, I have written poems for amusement. In 2014, I wrote my first book, *Blueberries and Bears and My Brother's Shoes*, a book about growing up in the forties and fifties. After I self-published it and gave it to friends and family to read, they encouraged me to get serious about my writing.

Willerton Woods is my seventh mystery novel. My dad hunted in the Upper Peninsula and we made yearly trips before hunting season to spruce up his deer blind.

Crossing Sydney was my first novel and it was published in July 2015. It has received outstanding reviews.

Don't Smother Your Mother, *A Bad Week in Hollister*, and *Floating Face Down*, are the Sheriff "Cowboy" Berkson series. I wavered a lot about the ending the series, as I knew it meant the end of writing about some of my favorite characters. However, I figured there are a lot of other people roaming around in my head that can wind up in a book. So, I sadly said goodbye to Cowboy and the cast of characters in the three-book series.

Let's Play Autopsy, my fourth book, takes place in Kalispell, Montana. The persons and places are fictitious, although at one time in my life when I was quite young, I did live in that city.

Cowtown is my sixth mystery novel. It takes place in a made-up Chicago neighborhood. The Campanales are an unusual family, who mistakenly think they are more qualified to take care of the town bully than the cops. Never a good idea, as they soon find out in this exciting story with an unexpected ending.

I never thought that, at the age of 76, I would become an author. I have set a goal for myself to write at least ten books before I die. I guess I better stick with it because you just never know.

I certainly am enjoying my retirement knowing, when I get up each morning, I have something to look forward to. You can find out more about me and my books at www.susanlpare.com. Please visit me there and feel free to send me your comments.